OPTIONAL PRACTICAL TRAINING

OPTIONAL PRACTICAL TRAINING

A Novel

SHUBHA SUNDER

Graywolf Press

Published by Graywolf Press
212 Third Avenue North, Suite 485
Minneapolis, Minnesota 55401

www.graywolfpress.org

Published in the United States of America
Printed in Canada

ISBN 978-1-64445-324-7 (paperback)
ISBN 978-1-64445-325-4 (ebook)

2 4 6 8 9 7 5 3 1
First Graywolf Printing, 2025

Library of Congress Cataloging-in-Publication Data

Names: Sunder, Shubha, 1982– author.
Title: Optional practical training : a novel / Shubha Sunder.
Description: Minneapolis, Minnesota : Graywolf Press, 2025.
Identifiers: LCCN 2024035480 (print) | LCCN 2024035481 (ebook) |
    ISBN 9781644453247 (trade paperback ; acid-free paper) | ISBN
    9781644453254 (epub)
Subjects: LCGFT: Novels.
Classification: LCC PS3619.U5623 O68 2025 (print) | LCC PS3619.U5623
    (ebook) | DDC 813/.6—dc23/eng/20240809
LC record available at https://lccn.loc.gov/2024035480
LC ebook record available at https://lccn.loc.gov/2024035481

Cover design: Kimberly Glyder

To Navi and Bill

The term "immigrant" means every alien except . . . (J) an alien having a residence in a foreign country which he has no intention of abandoning who is a bona fide student, scholar, trainee, teacher . . . in a field of specialized knowledge or skill.

—Immigration and Nationality Act of 1965

OPTIONAL PRACTICAL TRAINING

PART I

CHAPTER ONE

There was this immigrant man, the landlord told me, Indian, like you, who came to this country around the time of the First World War and wanted to become a citizen. He was Sikh. He had a long beard and a turban, and his lawyer had to convince an immigration judge he was white, since only white immigrants were allowed citizenship back then.

Was he fair skinned? I asked.

The landlord, a professorial type with his round spectacles, corduroy jacket, and assortment of mail tucked under his arm like a stack of student papers, seemed pleased by my question, as if I had raised my hand in class and said something insightful. What this episode in American history had highlighted for him was not so much his country's racist past—of that he had always been well aware—but rather, the tricky concept of race itself. How do we define it? The lawyer's previous client had been a Japanese man, and during that trial the lawyer—who was himself, needless to say, white—had placed a hand alongside his client's to demonstrate the similarity between the foreigner's skin color and his own. But the judge was unconvinced. You're not white, he told the Japanese man, you're Oriental. So, for his Indian client, the lawyer was forced to try a different tack. This man is of high birth, he said to the court. In his society members of the noble Brahmin caste look down on darker, lower castes the same way we whites in America look down on the Negroes. Therefore, he is one of us and should be given citizenship.

Are you Brahmin? the landlord asked me, pronouncing the *a* sound as if he were saying "apple." We were standing in the wood-paneled foyer of his building in Cambridge. I had come to see the apartment I'd found listed on an online forum the previous week, a time when I'd still been a college student, living on the small, tranquil campus outside Philadelphia that had for the last four years, since 2002, been my home in America.

I spent a lot of time in India, he continued. Delhi, mostly, but also Goa, at a hippie commune. I was in an altered state much of that time, I might add. It was the seventies, after all.

In our email exchange, the landlord had been terse, stating only that the apartment was available starting in August and that he would see me there May 18 at 8:00 a.m. I'd wondered if I had put him off by describing who I was and my reasons for moving to Boston, but now it seemed clear he was a congenial sort, just not over email.

I remember, he went on, how the matrimonial columns in Indian newspapers used terms like "wheatish" and "dusky" to describe women's complexions. Is it still like that?

I said it very much was and that Fair & Lovely cream, which he might have seen advertised alongside those personal columns, remained a popular product.

Remind me, he said, you're a graduate student, yes?

High school teacher, I said. Math and physics.

That's right, he said. I remember now.

He led the way up a staircase that, like the paneling in the foyer, was of dark, rich wood. From the sidewalk, the building resembled a large house. But inside it was obvious how the doors—two on each landing with brass numerals—were entrances to separate flats. The steps creaked as we ascended, and the sound thrilled me, as if I were climbing a formidable mountain, hearing the footsteps of those who had gone before. On the third level, he produced a key and revealed a bright studio apartment slightly larger than the dorm room

I'd vacated the previous evening before taking the overnight train to Boston, with a stove and sink against one wall, and a bay window facing the street. Eleven hundred a month, he said. Heat and hot water included. If you don't like the furniture, I can remove it.

I said I would find the furniture useful, since I had none of my own.

It's an international community here, he went on, leaning against the doorframe with his hand on his hip. There's a Harvard postdoc downstairs, an anthropologist from Colombia. I was an anthropology major, too, in college. Never imagined then that I'd end up in real estate. He looked at the ceiling and shook his head in wonder. When I bought this building twenty years ago, it was a mess. I had visiting scholars from Africa and from China say, We thought America was supposed to be a first world country—why are these places like third world dwellings? People who want to bring back rent control forget how embarrassing some of those properties were.

I walked to the bay window and looked out at the view. The rent would be almost half my monthly pay.

What do you think? he asked me. It's nice, isn't it? You'll like the neighborhood, too, I have no doubt. There's an Indian restaurant right around the corner. And Christina's further down. Fantastic selection of spices. The young woman down the hallway is a musician, from Latvia or Estonia, I forget which. She performs regularly at the Lilypad, next to Bukowski, where my discussion group meets.

At the group's last gathering, he said, a participant said she couldn't help despising the Sikh man for the move his lawyer made in court. She'd known a Sikh kid growing up, known that his parents had fled India, where they'd been harassed and threatened for being Sikh. The kid was a junior in college on 9/11, and a week after the attacks he was accosted on the street and pummeled by a pair of white guys. They thought his turban meant he was Muslim—they said this in their police statement, as if, had he been what they thought, their actions would have been justified. It disgusts me, the woman said, when members of different oppressed groups, instead of banding together, become caught in a competition to see who could be "more white."

She had to remind herself that there was a larger issue at play, that the Sikh man was essentially trapped. He had to claim he was white because that's what the system demanded. And though these systems are created by people, they become like air and water—they're all around and within us. When an individual acts a certain way, we jump to ascribe his actions to his character, forgetting that, like iron filings bending to a magnetic field, those actions are governed by systemic laws. But where's the question of free will then? someone in the group asked. Are you saying this Sikh guy, presumably of sound mind, could not recognize the perverseness of the case his lawyer was making?

It wasn't the first time, the landlord said as he led me back down the stairs, that the discussion group had found themselves talking about free will. So many questions seemed to lead to the possibility that everything, all our choices, were predetermined. I believe, he said, it's a question you physicists tackle as well, yes?

I wouldn't really call myself a physicist, I said, since all I had was a bachelor's degree in the subject and a teaching certificate.

On the front porch, we stood surrounded by rain, curtains of water rippling over the lawn and its border of thick-leaved shrubs, obscuring the street and the houses facing us. My mind felt clear. I wanted the apartment. It was the bay window that convinced me. Broad sill; tall, bright panes: already I could picture myself sitting for hours in that nook, coffee and writing journal at hand. My dorm room had had a similar setup, with a trapezoidal bench fitted to the angles of the window, looking out over a tree-lined pond and, behind it, the president's mansion, whose slate roof turned rosy on clear evenings as the sun went down, a smaller, paler, gentler sun than I'd grown up beneath in India.

You're here on a green card? the landlord asked, raising his voice over the sound of the rain. He was a tall man, well over six feet, with long, straight limbs and a slight potbelly pushing at the buttons of his corduroy jacket. His eyes had the darting quality of a bird's, and his lips kept puckering in an expression of mild amusement.

I told him I was still on a student visa, that once I started my teaching job I would be in OPT status. Optional practical training. It was valid for one year. After that I'd have to get a work visa. But the school would sponsor me. The school where I'd be teaching.

Will you go back to India at some point, do you think, or stay here?

I don't know for sure yet, I said. My plan for the next few years was to teach at the school and, in my spare time, write. I had begun a novel in college and intended to finish it as soon as I could.

The landlord smirked, then nodded, as if he didn't want to be the one to tell me my plans were fanciful. Everything is before you, he said. Let me know by tonight if you're interested.

■

At Café Rustica on Beacon Street, I took off my drenched canvas shoes and placed them under my chair, along with my socks and the collapsed, dripping umbrella I'd wrestled against the wind on my walk from the landlord's. My backpack and suitcase were also wet, but my passport and papers, I was relieved to find, had stayed dry in their plastic folders. As I was rolling up the cuffs of my soaked jeans, Theta arrived. There's this vortex in Canada, she said, sucking in tons of chilled air from the ocean. Coldest spring on record.

She shook out her raincoat, grimacing as if the water drops scattering from it smelled foul. I can't believe I have another three years to go. I've thought about quitting the program just to get away from the weather. It's making me depressed, it's making me sick. But my dad would kill me if I quit. He'd say, I came as a refugee, I came to escape *genocide*, and you're fleeing from what? The snow? Go buy yourself some mittens and stop whining.

She folded her thin body into the seat across from me, knees to chest, and I was reminded of how she used to brush her teeth in our dormitory bathroom: wrapped in a towel, balanced on one foot with the other beneath her like a heron. She'd been a senior my freshman year and one of the first people to welcome me when I arrived from

India. She was glad to see me, she said now, glad I'd gotten in touch. On the walk over, she'd thought about what a different person she'd been in college: an extrovert, a bringer-together of people. The mere thought of attending a party these days, let alone organizing one, made her want to lie down from exhaustion. She blamed the weather more than her doctoral program. She'd grown up in New Zealand and Oregon, and in both places her body had always felt at one with the temperature. Cool, fresh, stable. The Northeast was a different story. Starting in college, she'd been plagued by tension headaches and bouts of acid reflux, symptoms she'd assumed were due to other things: dining hall food, academic stress, the need, particular to our college, to show up to every single late-night party so you wouldn't be labeled a nerd. These days, in summer, the hot, sticky air turned her body into a heat trap. By early October, while others were out picking apples and enjoying the foliage, she had to stay indoors and drink glasses of water, fifteen or more a day, to douse the fires raging beneath her skin. For about three weeks in the fall, she said, I feel good. Then when the deep cold kicks in and the darkness to go with it, I turn rigid. My muscles become stone. It must be an even bigger challenge for you, the winters, coming from India.

I told her that I'd suffered from asthma through my childhood and adolescence in Bangalore, that within a day or two of arriving in America I'd stopped wheezing. Orientation week was the first time in my life I could properly fill my lungs.

Amazing, she said, shaking her head. Amazing that you had to come here in order to breathe. Let's get a drink. My treat.

As we sipped our lattes, hers made with soy milk, she told me she was avoiding dairy to see if that would help her temperature regulation. She'd gone off wheat, too, with her now-former boyfriend, a guy from rural Vermont who'd tried to convince her that living in the city didn't allow her to fully experience the glories of winter. In February, he'd taken her up a mountain not far from his family home. I assumed, she said, that I'd be on the bunny slopes with an instructor while he skied the advanced trails, but no, he wanted us to hike up this remote path to the very top, way past the ski lift. And he didn't even bring skis—just this flimsy plastic sled, not much more than those trays we used to steal from the dining hall to ride down Radnor Hill. He strapped it over his backpack. He looked like a red turtle. He gave me these tights to wear under my insulated pants and this face mask he said would keep me warm no matter what. For the first half it was bearable. Then my toes started to go numb. Wait till we get to the top, he said. Just wait. You'll feel this amazing surge, better than sex. My legs were starting to cramp, and my hands, too. I tried taking small steps and large steps, tried breathing all kinds of different ways. Wait till we get to the top, he kept saying. Then you'll understand. You'll understand everything. Nature will throw everything at you, and you'll come through.

Well, we get closer to the top and the wind is so ridiculous I can feel it lifting me off the ground. And he's acting more and more excited. I can see less and less because now there's fog—or maybe we're high enough that the fog is actually cloud. I see what I think is him a few feet ahead of me, and I try to focus on the little pocket of warm air around my nose, held in place by the mask. Soon I'm bent double, charging the wind like a bull, angry as hell. With him, with myself for following along. I fall a couple of times, scrabble, get snow in my mask. And all of a sudden I realize I'm going downhill, the fog is clearing, the wind is no longer knocking me over. I can't see my boyfriend anywhere. I tell myself he's just ahead, even though I know he's probably behind, searching frantically for me. I can't make my feet turn around. I'm in the grip of something—not exhilaration, not desperation, just a state of perpetual motion, like when I hit my running stride and feel I can go forever. By the time I got to the bottom, my fingers, toes, and the tops of my ears were frostbitten.

A pair of skiers, packing up their car, had gawked at her as she approached. She made her accent extra British—as people like her and me did in situations when we had to prove we were sophisticated. Excuse me, so sorry to disturb, I'm in a bit of a fix here, you see, my friend and I got separated. If there's any way you can give me a ride into town, I'd be e-ver so grateful.

I'm used to being the only non-white person around, she said, but this couple was something else—they made me feel like a rare animal escaped from the zoo. On the drive, they said things like, Your English is so good—where are you from? No, where are you *from*? Where are your parents from? Is Theta a Cambodian name? No, I said, my father wanted me to be a mathematician. And for them this was the most incredible thing they'd ever heard. It was like I was supposed to have grown up in a jungle with monkeys. They gave me their phone number, told me to call them the next time I was in the area. They'd have me over to their house, they said, they would put me up in their guest bedroom. They were part of this dinner group, which every month had a different theme. Last month was Sweden, this month was Mexico, guess what it would be when I visited? They didn't even ask me if I cooked Cambodian food, or if I liked to cook at all. They just said, We can't take too much spice—you'd have to turn down the heat.

Theta's voice had grown shrill, her elfin features contorted into a snarl, and I was reminded of the evening when we'd been part of a group attending a dance in the city—an event for Philadelphia-area international students, held in a building with a high rotunda and balconies overlooking the Schuylkill River. On our walk back to the train station, a man driving by shouted something from the window of his car. I didn't catch the words—my ears were still ringing from the thumping dance music—but I surmised from what the others were saying that he'd told us we didn't belong here. Theta's reaction was louder and angrier than anyone else's—overblown, I couldn't help thinking, in light of the grand reception we'd just been given, hundreds of us foreigners from across the world; it was all warmth and camaraderie as we danced and bounced around a six-foot-high inflated globe, but to her all of this meant nothing in the face of a fleeting encounter with a disgruntled stranger.

She propped her elbows on the table and covered her face with her hands. My boyfriend was right, she continued, speaking through the gap between her palms. Climbing that mountain did make me understand everything. I realized I don't want to adjust to this place. Dealing with white people is hard enough, dealing with white people and being miserable with the weather just isn't worth it.

Outside the rain had lessened, but the sky was still overcast, which made the hanging lamps in the café seem extra cheerful. The brick walls glowed, and I envisioned, on fine days, walking here from my studio apartment to have a drink and write. I retrieved my socks and sodden canvas shoes and started to pull them on. I'd worn the shoes for the last four years, I told Theta. Through the winters. My feet had been chilly, but I'd learned to swallow something hot before venturing outside and then walk as briskly as I could to work up a sweat. I'd never felt like an outsider at college, not in a bad way. On the contrary, I'd felt welcomed from the very beginning, pampered even. There were moments when I couldn't believe my good fortune at having been allowed to come here.

She leaned forward as if about to admonish me but then seemed to rethink what she'd planned to say. So, have you found an apartment?

I believe I have, I said. A room of one's own, so to speak.

How much will you be paying?

I told her, and her mouth opened in shock. Make sure you have enough left, she said, to buy a pair of winter boots. Cambridge sidewalks in January are the freaking tundra.

■

I paused outside Porter Square Station, in my wet clothes, to observe what a sign there called a kinetic sculpture—three elevated red objects shaped like tongues, tumbling about their axes and orbiting a tall white pole. My thoughts circled back to Theta's shocked expression at my rent, which led me to review my predicted costs—food, transportation, utilities—and wonder if I'd overlooked something. After a brief trance, I descended a long escalator to the commuter rail platform and boarded the train to Wilton. Soon I was passing the same backyards and open spaces I'd sped by in March, no longer barren and covered with dirty snow, but green, with that profusion of young spring leaves I associated with Impressionist paintings. A pond slid into view, its edges blurred by clumps of reeds. The rain started again. It drew long diagonal streaks across the windows. Anyone want to get off at Brandeis? the conductor called as she strode up the aisle. That was a question, she added cheerfully. Not a threat.

At Wilton, I alighted and took shelter in one of the covered seating areas to study the map I'd printed the morning before, on my final visit to the college library before departing campus. When I'd come to interview for the teaching position two months earlier, the science department head had picked me up at the platform. Today, for my meeting with the human resources director, I would be on my own. I waited for the rain to stop, and soon the sun, as if just for me, broke through the clouds and turned the last of the falling drops to bright, scattered lines that crisscrossed in midair.

I traversed the main road and walked past a meadow where a solitary deer stood grazing amid small white flowers that dotted the grass like snow. The hill was steep, and I started to sweat. I took my jacket off and tied it around the handle of my suitcase. The houses, half hidden by tall hedges, were large and sprawling, with broad driveways occupied by three, sometimes four cars. Frequently, the sidewalk dissolved into weeds, forcing me into the road. I checked my watch: I had twenty minutes, enough time to find a bathroom and neaten my hair before my appointment. At the campus gate, with its painted wooden sign bearing the school's name and logo, I paused to put my jacket back on, to hide my creased blouse. My own high school had been a single stone structure with small windows divided by vertical grilles. Here there was a central square of lawn surrounded by low buildings, all painted yellow and red. I felt the sweat soaking my clothes. A student was striding across the lawn in frayed shorts and a T-shirt, whistling a tune as her ponytail bobbed and swung. She looked more confident than I'd ever felt as a teenager, and suddenly

I resented her, this girl I didn't know, for never having to wear a tie and blazer in the heat or be stopped and reprimanded for whistling. I waved and asked if she could direct me to Lila MacDonald.

She eyed me curiously, pointing to one of the buildings. Basement, she called, next to the bookstore, before resuming her whistling.

■

In the business office, Lila, a pallid, heavyset woman, collected my forms, still dry in their plastic folder, and handed me a manila envelope thick with more papers. Here's your OPT stuff, she said. The lawyers told me everything's in order, but I'd still go through it all and make sure they've got your details right. Filing has gotten trickier lately, as you can imagine.

The air-conditioning in Lila's office was supercooling my wet clothes. She herself was wearing a cardigan made of a red feathery material, a color and texture similar to that of her hair, cut in layers around her square face. A private school down the road, she went on, hired a Pakistani man last year. English speaking, fully qualified, just like you. But when he went home for the summer and showed up at the American consulate in Pakistan with his passport and visa application, they found a small discrepancy—a wrong date or spelling error—and rejected him. That's why I'd double-check everything if I were you, honey.

I reminded her that I didn't have to visit a consulate this summer since I already had a visa and it was valid for another year, until 2007. OPT was just an adjustment of status.

Yes, honey, and you're a woman. And you're from India—I know there are Muslims there, but it's not like Iran, say, or Iraq. Besides, you're such a sweet, tiny thing—how could anyone suspect you of being a threat? She laughed and reached across her desk to pat my arm. She wore multiple rings on her fingers, with gems so large and heavy looking I wondered how she could type. Her son, she said, had recently married an Indian woman. Lila had never liked Indian food—the chili peppers gave her terrible heartburn, so when she and her husband visited their daughter-in-law's family in Detroit, she'd taken along quantities of crackers and peanut butter, thinking she might otherwise starve. Her son's mother-in-law, an Ayurvedic doctor, had, after hearing of her ailments, performed a thorough examination. Looked at her eyes, her skin, her hair, asked about her sleeping patterns, her energy at various times of day, things that no American physician had ever bothered with. My dosha, she said, is apparently a combination of heat and cold. You must know all the names, yes? For these balances of energy. She moved her ring-studded hands up and down. Her daughter-in-law's mother had made this meal that was nothing like the Indian food she'd eaten at restaurants. It was spicy—she could see the red chili peppers floating in oil—but when she mixed things the way she'd been told, it was nowhere near as hot as she'd imagined. And she felt fine afterward—no acid reflux, no rosacea. She watched the Indian woman cook and was blown away by how she used just one little steel cup to measure everything—rice, lentils, flour, milk. A pinch of this, a sprinkle of that. No timers, no thermometers, no scales. Mixed everything with her hands, lifted hot flatbreads off an open flame with her fingertips. I'm looking at you now, she said, and you're making me hungry, reminding me of all that great Indian food. Do you have any questions, honey?

I asked, abruptly but as politely as I could, if she'd tell me what my take-home pay would be each month.

Of course, honey, just give me a minute. Let's assume standard health insurance, dental, and base retirement contribution. She picked up a calculator. Her rings flashed as she punched the keys. Then she read out a number that left me deflated.

■

Outside Lila's office, in the empty corridor, I called the landlord, left a halting message, then stared at the floor for several moments, until the sound of footsteps made me look up. Stephanie, a science teacher

I'd met in March, was brushing chalk dust off the sleeve of her black frock. She was a straight-backed woman with a brisk stride, here to escort me to lunch. Her flat yellow hair, pulled tight against her scalp, was secured in a small knot at the top of her head, high above the stiff collar of her dress. She had a prominent jaw and an intense gaze, through spectacles whose frames were of a bright, almost fluorescent pink. Simultaneously humorous and severe, I thought, a useful impression for a teacher to give her students.

She tilted her head back toward Lila's door as we left. Did she talk your ear off? When Andy said your first meeting of the day was with her, I thought, Don't be surprised if our new teacher changes her mind about joining us. The other day I heard her ask Marie if she could touch her hair—Marie, who's Jamaican. I mean, seriously, in 2006?

Andy, she went on, would be joining us in the cafeteria. He'd been dealing all morning with a student's mother, a woman who had made a significant donation to the school's endowment and earned a reputation, in the science department at least, for being something of a lunatic. Her son, a sweet, dreamy sort of kid, was failing chemistry. The department had recommended he enroll in a less quantitative course: ecosystems, for example, or animal behavior. But his mother dismissed the idea, saying courses like those would make her son's transcript look like he was too stupid or too lazy to take real chemistry. Now that he was heading for an F, she'd concluded not that the course had been a bad choice for her son but that he'd been unfairly graded. His scores on lab reports and tests did not reflect his intelligence, she insisted, because accommodations had not been made for his learning style, which was more kinesthetic than oral or visual, as had been documented by a specialist in the fifty-page report that she distributed to his teachers at the start of each term. Written assignments were especially challenging for him, so why hadn't the chemistry teacher figured out alternative ways to measure her child's understanding? Writing and performing a song, for example? Or making a sculpture? She demanded that his grade be changed.

Don't get me started on grades, Stephanie said, raising a defensive palm. If he were in the C range—C's the new F these days, that's a different matter—if he were getting, say, a solid C plus, then Andy might consent to bump it up to a B minus. Since it's an F, I predict he'll let him submit test corrections or do an extra project to get into the D range, and then we'll put a P on his transcript so it looks like he'd signed up for a pass-fail course—which technically, yes, he would've had to do at the beginning of the year, but this might be the only way to get the mom off our backs. What's your philosophy on grades?

We were walking back across the central lawn, around groups of students picnicking in the grass. When I was at school, it was expressly forbidden to eat on the playground, where eagles would swoop down and snatch food from our fingers, often drawing blood with their talons.

I said I'd grown up in a very different sort of educational system, one in which grades were, like rules, immutable. Stephanie nodded, the muscles of her jaw flexing. It wasn't clear whether she approved of what I'd said or was merely noting it.

We found Andy, the head of the science department, sitting morosely on the edge of a table. I'd last spoken to him in April, when he'd called to tell me how delighted he was to offer me the position. Now he apologized for not having been able to give me a lift from the train station.

We were just talking about Niko and his mom, Stephanie said to him. Let me guess, pass-fail?

As Andy lowered his gray, shaggy head and started speaking to the floor, I recalled the impression of him that I'd had at my interview: a rumpled, mild-tempered, slightly clumsy beast of burden, whose gentleness and dependability made him both an object of affection and the butt of jokes among those he served. No one's asking if college is the right choice for this kid, he said. His mom has a list of where she wants him to apply. I wanted to tell her, What your son needs is a year in the Peace Corps. Something to jolt him out of his bubble. When I was eighteen, I went to Kenya and worked in a village there for ten months—built houses and taught kids English. I'd never been to a developing country before. It changed my life.

He glanced up at me, and looked momentarily confused. Now did you grow up here or in India?

Bangalore, I said, speaking over clattering dishes and other conversations. The cafeteria, its cavernous ceiling crossed by wooden beams and hung with various countries' flags, was an echo chamber.

Moving to the US must have been an adjustment, yes? Andy said as he offered me a tray.

I said I'd been shocked, working in the dining hall during freshman year of college, to be throwing away so much food at the end of each meal—food that was perfectly good, tossed into black plastic bags or poured down the sink. At home, if I spilled milk while drinking from a tumbler, my mother would dab her fingers in the puddle on the table and then against the rim of the glass to let the drops run down the inside edge. The first time I scraped out half a pan of lasagna, a pan so heavy it needed to be propped against the edge of the bin, I'd felt a wave of nausea, but after a few weeks I grew to relish it. So much excess, so much sheer waste. It must have been the sick glee a rich person would feel burning money.

Andy nodded gravely. We had an all-school discussion last year, he said, about food waste. A group of students raised the funds for a composter and had it installed to keep kitchen scraps out of the trash. I believe it's still being used.

Two steaming vats of soup, one red, one white, sat alongside a heap of bread bowls. I ladled cream of tomato into a hollow crust whose innards I assumed had been fed to the composter. Behind me, Andy was accosted by a blue-haired girl in expensive-looking boots. Her face was streaked with mascara, and she was hugging herself with bare, tattooed arms. Andy listened patiently as the girl ranted and stamped her foot, and I watched how freely and fully a student could throw a fit before a teacher and be treated with kindness. Stephanie leaned toward me and spoke in a whisper. Don't get me wrong, I love

Andy. And the kids love him. He's a teddy bear. Wrong person in many ways for department head—too sensitive, too scared of conflict. My instinct whenever I'm having a problem is to sort it out myself instead of troubling him. How was the apartment hunt, by the way? Did you find a place?

I'd seen one that morning, I told her, but it was likely to be outside my budget.

Likely? she said, frowning. Didn't they tell you the rent?

I said I was waiting for a return call.

Make sure it's legit. There's every kind of quack around town. My friend's sister rented a place in Somerville where the heat almost never worked and the water in the shower came out orange.

She led me to a table where two teachers, a man and a woman, were eating side by side.

Keith, the man said, waving a paint-stained hand. Art department.

I'm Sharanya, the woman said. English and history.

Sharanya and I observed each other. A large, queenly presence in a silk kurta and gold bangles, she looked my mother's age. From across the table, I could smell her perfume. It was sandalwood, a scent I hadn't encountered in many months.

Pavitra is from Bangalore, Stephanie said to her.

Oh, beautiful city, Bangalore, Sharanya said, beaming. So green, so lush. I've been there only once, more than thirty years ago. We took the train from Bombay, my cousins and I. Nothing like overnight train journeys in India, the best way to see the country. And arriving in Bangalore, to all those blooming flowers and wonderful bakeries—it was heaven. There was this German botanist, you know, Krumbiegel. He was hired by the maharaja in Bangalore—part of the kingdom of Mysore at the time—to choose which trees to plant along the city's avenues. At all times of year, the maharaja said, I want something to be flowering. And of course, with the south Indian climate, all kinds of tropical and subtropical species can flourish. When I was there, the jacaranda and cassia were in full bloom. Magnificent, just magnificent.

Stephanie and Keith nodded, impressed, and glanced at me for confirmation. In the face of Sharanya's ebullience, I didn't feel inclined to spoil her memory of Bangalore by pointing out that in the years since her last visit, many of the trees had been cut down to clear the way for high-rises.

She kept talking. The colors in India, they're brighter and richer than anywhere. I was born in England and didn't travel abroad until I was six. When my parents and I arrived in Bombay, it was like that moment in *The Wizard of Oz*. My life until then was so gray and dreary, and all of a sudden I entered a new world full of color.

My cell phone rang. I apologized to everyone, stepped away from the table, and stammered hello to the landlord. I thanked him again for taking the time to see me that morning. I liked the apartment very much, and I would be a good, responsible tenant. Then I asked him if there was any way he could offer it to me at a rent lower than what he'd quoted. I saw the bay window in my mind's eye and felt my voice shake as I spoke. He did not interrupt me. I heard horns beeping in the background and imagined him driving or walking down a busy road. When I finished, he said he understood my position but could not, unfortunately, help me.

I hung up and walked to the far end of the cafeteria, where I found myself staring at a map of the world pinned to the wall. The land borders of India, which as a teenager I'd learned to sketch freehand, looked alien to me in this international drawing, which described a shrunken, misshapen territory, with Kashmir decapitated.

You'll be the only one next year, a voice said, and I turned to find Sharanya behind me. She was retiring in June, she said, after more than twenty years as the lone Indian faculty member. A decade ago, she'd organized a school assembly in honor of Diwali, and it had been such a hit—costumes, music, lights—that she'd been asked to do it every year since. What had started as a simple impulse to stand up and say, Here's what's important to me, let me share it with you, had turned into a burden: Why am I *expected* to take this on? But she'd always given in, partly because it felt like a duty—we were, after all, ambassadors in a place like this—and partly because if an American-born teacher organized a Diwali event, Sharanya would be driven mad by their horrendous pronunciation of Sanskrit names and her revived awareness of Westerners trampling, as they were wont to do, on sacred cultures and traditions. It's a delicate balance, she said, educating them without conveying the impression that what's ours is now theirs. My advice is to make it all as personal as possible. Tell them how you and your family celebrate Diwali.

Vaguely, for the landlord's response had sent my thoughts into a whirl, I said that Sankranti, not Diwali, was my family's main festival.

Oh, nobody will know what that is, she said. And I wouldn't recommend taking on more than one assembly.

When I returned to my spot at the table, my soup in its bread bowl was starting to congeal. Through the fog in my head, I heard Stephanie tell me they were discussing the fate of a group of international students, all Korean, who'd beaten up an American student, one of Keith's advisees. The American student was of Korean descent. He'd refused, apparently, to address the Korean boys with a term of respect, and that was what had led to the beating.

I still can't get all the details out of him, Keith said, a look of fascination on his face, which was round and boyish in spite of the stubble lining his jaw. The kid showed up to my office covered in bruises and claimed it was seasonal allergies—that he'd been rubbing his eyes too hard. But I refused to let him go until he let me know what had actually happened, and then he begged me not to tell anyone. No one would understand, he said. The Korean boys would see him as a traitor; his American friends would form a bad impression of Korean culture. I said, Look, we're a community. We can't let people go around beating others up. Now he's furious at me for having reported the boys. And to be honest, I'm starting to regret the decision. Keith leaned forward. His hushed voice grew even softer as he said he'd been summoned that morning to Marissa's office. She was packing her briefcase the whole time I was there. Off to some fundraising event on the West Coast. How she can call herself principal when she's never on campus, I don't know. Anyway, she thinks their punishment should be a forfeiture of a weekend trip! I wanted to say, If a group of white students had beaten up another white student—or a Black student—they'd be suspended or worse. But she frames it as a question of cultural misunderstanding, and it's obvious why. They come from wealthy business families, many of these kids. Their parents effectively finance the school—without their money, we'd be in a hole. He straightened up, cleared his throat, and resumed his normal voice. I have complicated feelings about our international-student program. How any family can send their children halfway around the world at such a young age. He looked at me. How old were you when you came here?

Eighteen, I said.

He nodded sympathetically. I know a woman from Quebec who came to Boston when she was your age. She's been here several decades now, but her head still hurts at night from thinking and speaking in English all day. When she hears a French song, she cries.

I recalled my college campus, its stone buildings and elegant willow trees, and longed to be back in my dorm room with my books. Under the collective gaze of my companions, I took a spoonful of soup and held it in my mouth.

So, tell us, Keith said, what made you decide to teach?

My throat muscles moved, and the soup went down. I'd been a teaching assistant, I said, in the physics department, and before that, as far back as I could remember, I'd always enjoyed teaching. When I was a girl, my classmates would come to me for help with homework.

I'd used these words before, in interviews, on my teaching application. Now they felt like someone else's. I prodded my soggy bread bowl with a spoon and watched it collapse into itself.

■

Dragging my suitcase, I crossed the now-deserted lawn. Through a window above me came a chorus of bored voices: Je sais, tu sais, il/elle/on sait. I remembered the monotony of my own school days.

When I reached the dirt path leading to the main road, my phone rang. It was the landlord. I have a proposal for you, he said. I like to do what I can to help people. I've been sitting in my office thinking, What can I do for this nice young woman from India who's just starting out in Boston?

I pictured him behind his desk: corduroy jacket draped over the back of a swivel chair where he sat like a professor holding office hours. His mother, he went on, lived two blocks from the apartment he'd shown me that morning. She was in her nineties and had a bad leg. The man who'd lived on the third floor, a long-term lodger, was moving out, and the landlord had decided to postpone renovating the place, since his mother would not tolerate workers in the house. It's a bit run-down, mind you. And there's no private kitchen—you'd need to go downstairs to cook. But you can have it for, let's say six hundred a month.

Does it have windows? I asked.

There was a small window facing the street, he said, and a medium-sized bay window overlooking the side yard. The radiators were old and weak. The bathroom was functional, as long as I didn't mind loose fittings and a bit of rust. Chipped plaster, cracked tiles. The kind of thing one expects in an old house.

I imagined the bay window and the trees beyond, and my heart lifted. With the phone still held to my ear, I unzipped my jacket. The wind was picking up. It felt warm against my rumpled blouse.

I had a place to come back to and was ready to fly home.

PART II

CHAPTER **TWO**

I took an auto-rickshaw to Brigade Road, then walked up Church Street to King's. The place hadn't changed: smoky lamps, uneven cave-like walls, windows draped with woven-cane blinds. Ajit was waiting at a corner table and sprang to his feet when he saw me, his teeth and the whites of his eyes gleaming wetly in the dimness. Long hair suits you, he said, reaching out and tugging at a strand that had escaped my ponytail. Oh sorry, was that too much? I've just been lonely for a long time, you see. All my close friends have moved away, and those who are still here I don't get together with very often. They think I've changed since my episode last year. Which I have, obviously, but I'm fundamentally the same person—reserved, humorous, philosophical.

His laugh combined a lopsided smile and a snort, and I smelled on his breath the Hajmola candies we used to chew while holding hands on park benches. His body was still gangly, his ribs still protruding, I imagined, beneath his shirt, but his face had filled out, the angles of his cheekbones and chin now blunted, his forehead thickened by a receding hairline. He was my age, twenty-two, but looked closer to thirty. Across the room, by the entrance, the restaurant owner lounged beside a mini television set playing a Bollywood film, its music half drowned by the clattering of dishes from the kitchen. The air was suffused by smells of naan and roasting meats. A busboy with a towel over his shoulder approached, and I ordered my favorites. Ajit added a biryani. You've lost weight, he told me. When was the last time we met? Was it two years ago? No, three. You were home for summer vacation. It was at Deepthi's party. I remember looking at you and thinking, Wow, she's growing fat. I relished it, to be quite honest, the fact that America had set you on the path to obesity. I wanted to say, This is what you get for going abroad, all you fools who think you're so great for getting into American universities with scholarships and all, you're turning into Humpty-Dumpties.

The busboy returned with two nimbu panis in copper-plated tumblers. Ajit tipped his head back and drank, his Adam's apple running up and down like an animal caught in a bag. I thought about how spitefulness never goes away in a person but hides beneath the surface and peeps out at odd moments. I looked away before Ajit could meet my gaze and saw that a couple with a child—a little boy four or five years old—were settling themselves at the table beside ours. The boy's head was wrapped in a monkey cap, and he was clasping to his chest a bright-red water bottle that he refused to give up as his mother tried to take his hand and guide him to a separate chair. Finally, she lifted him onto her lap, where he perched, sentinel like, his alert gaze traveling around the room until it met mine.

You should come to the gallery afterward, Ajit was saying. Ronnie will be there. I can introduce you if you want. People think he must be outgoing based on his cartoons, but actually he's very shy and awkward. The other day this lady came into the gallery and tried to flirt with him. Pleased to meet you, Ronnie dear, can you give me a tour of your little shop? I was dissolving with laughter, and Ronnie just stammered away and stared at her breasts. He had done so many caricatures of people like her, with all those hilarious details of the classic Anglo-Indian female: short curly hair, big teeth, tight-fitting polka-dot dress. And now she was standing right in front of him, like she had walked out of his sketchbook. Do you still have that poster I got you before you left?

I'd hung the poster, titled "Boomtown," in every dorm room I'd occupied in college. More than one visitor had pointed to a particular element in Ronnie's crowded drawing, a man on a motorcycle impaled by rods sticking out from the lorry in front of him, and asked if that kind of thing happened often on Indian streets.

It's sold lakhs of copies, did you know? Ajit went on. A household name now, Ronnie D'Souza. Our teachers thought he was autistic because he didn't like to speak—and when he did speak, it was in this monotone, like a robot. He still talks that way, mumbles more like. They wrote him off as stupid. Now they want to brag about him being a St Paul's graduate. They invite him to be the chief guest at annual days, and when he gives his halting speeches, they smile as if he's a great orator. A bizarre show—Father Francis pretending he and his staff loved Ronnie from the beginning, Ronnie going along with the whole charade. I asked him once why he doesn't just tell Father Francis, Fuck off, why should I do anything for you and your Dickensian school? His response surprised me. He said he was grateful, genuinely grateful to St Paul's for helping him become the successful artist that he is. I said, What the hell did they do for you? He said that once they decided he was not worth bothering with, they left him alone. They didn't torture him, didn't beat him. They let him be in his fantasy world. It's an absurd tendency we Indians have, don't you agree, this impulse toward gratitude? We think we deserve to be flogged, so when some authority figure decides not to flog us, we think he's great. And when we do get a flogging, we say it's for our own good. The British are still alive and well in our spirit.

He chuckled at his own proclamations. At our last visit here, four years ago, when he'd said that whatever respect he'd had for me he'd lost because I'd gone and done what was so predictable and within the means of any averagely intelligent, English-speaking Indian student—ingratiated myself to an American college so I could escape the inconveniences of my own, poor country—I'd put my share of the bill on the table and left the restaurant, resolved never to speak to him again. Since then, he'd emailed me several times, long-winded, semicoherent letters. Now he served me generous helpings from each of the steaming dishes that had been set before us, all served in shallow bowls, copper plated like our tumblers. The little boy in his monkey cap was still looking over at me. I'd blinked and smiled at him a few times, but his gaze remained serious. He slithered off his mother's lap and, with his water bottle tucked under his arm, strode over and touched my knee. For a moment I thought he was going to climb into my lap, but then he made a ninety-degree turn, looking over his shoulder as if he expected me to follow. His mother gestured and called to him several times before shaking her head in exasperation and resuming her meal.

Have you visited our beloved alma mater? Ajit said. I bet the teachers were thrilled to see you. What greater compliment than to have a student follow in their footsteps?

I didn't tell him my reception in the St Paul's staff room had been tepid. Why, one of my former teachers wanted to know, did I need to go to *America* of all places to become a *teacher* of all things? We had high hopes for you, another said. In our generation, women did not have so many opportunities, so we became teachers. But now? Through the grilles of the staff-room window I saw the playground below and the glinting glass shards cemented along the top of its high wall to keep us from climbing over. At lunch break we used to thunder like migrating buffalo onto the field, our feet kicking up dust that rose and hung over us in a reddish dome. We ran and screamed under the white-hot sun as if we were mad. It was our only release valve, lunch break: the rest of the day we sat in creaky chairs and jiggled our legs under our desks, forty-five to sixty of us sweating in the classroom as teachers came and went and admonished us for fidgeting.

We can go to Lalbagh for a walk if you want, Ajit said. I can drive us there.

I assumed he'd brought his brother's car, the one with the tinted windows whose privacy we used to avail ourselves of on isolated, dead-end streets. I always worried someone would see the vehicle rocking on its wheels and call the police, but the worst that happened was that a man in a Gandhi cap once rapped on the hood with his umbrella.

I'm supposed to get at least one hour of outdoor exercise a day, Ajit continued. Tough when I'm at the gallery till six. I want to leave that job—if it can even be called a job when Ronnie just needs someone to sit in the gallery so he can shut his studio door and make his cartoons. But doing nothing seems to be all I'm fit for. My parents think so, too. The other day I had an interview at an advertising agency. The woman asked why I hadn't completed my bachelor's, and I told her I took leave because I was having health problems. Her face made it clear she thought I was lazy. Annoying female—wearing a short-short skirt and a blazer, speaking very fast, with a Bombay accent, toting around her superior attitude. I pointed out the things I had done in college—theater productions, editing the student newspaper. I pulled out the limericks I'd written in high school, my piano certificate. I can compose a jingle on the spot, I told her, just give me a topic. We need proof you can work in a fast-paced environment, she said, and that was the end of the interview. If she'd given me the opportunity to make an ad in front of her, wouldn't that have shown my ability to work in a fast-paced environment? She reminded me of you a little bit, you know. You and your achiever mentality. Any assignment you were given, in any subject, you would blindly do it. So of course you come across as efficient, smart, an all-rounder. You and your like have no patience or sympathy for people like me, people who have specific talents, in poetry, in music, talents that our blessed Indian educational system does not recognize.

The little boy had come back around. He paused a few feet from our table and slurped from his water bottle, his small, wet mouth moving up and down the plastic spout in a vaguely vulgar way. His mother beckoned distractedly to him. She seemed young—not much older than I was—and deep in conversation with the man across from her. Ajit went on. Sorry, I don't mean to criticize you. You know I admire your focus. My mother always said I should think of you as a role model. She says hello, by the way. She's at a lunch party for P. K. Mohan—his seventy-fifth birthday. Rumors are he'll be closing up the bookshop by the end of the year. Such a tragedy. Where else in the world are you going to find a shop like that? My brother did a cruise in Norway last year with his wife, and he said the fjords made him think of Mohan Books. Walls, pillars of ice towering above you, with these narrow, tight passageways through them. No obvious logic to the way the books are arranged. And the fact that you can ask Mohan for any book and he'll know exactly where it is. I remember that short story you wrote in English class, about how the assistant disappears through the hole in the shop's ceiling to retrieve a book and ends up in an alternate universe. I read it and thought, Wow, I never would have expected you of all people to come up with a story like this. That was when I first felt attracted to you. Before that, you were just this boring, studious person with no creativity or imagination. Are you still writing?

I said the main reason I'd accepted the teaching job in Boston was so I'd have time to write. Through the corner of my eye, I saw the little boy inching closer to us again. He was still drinking, now holding his water bottle like a clarinet, elbows flared. When he was at my knee again, I asked him his name. A line of drool stretched from his lips to the spout as he stared with his large, glistening eyes. I wished I could reach over to the woolen monkey cap, which looked to be itchy and too warm, and pull it off his head.

Little terrorist, Ajit remarked. The boy turned to him and watched as Ajit shoveled biryani into his mouth. Then he pointed his bottle and sent a jet of water straight into Ajit's face.

■

In his email to me, which I didn't see until I was back in Boston, Ajit said that despite everything—our disagreements, our conflicting values and priorities, the fact that fortune had smiled on me and not on him, and the geographical distance between us, a distance he assumed would be permanent, given the unlikelihood that someone like me would ever care to return to India, coupled with his determination, as a staunch desi, never to abandon his country—we should still be friends. If his episode the previous year had taught him anything, it was never to take what he had for granted. Throughout his teenage years he had woken up with energy and a sense of well-being; now that those things had been snatched away, he wished he'd appreciated more his period of unadulterated good health. Similarly, our friendship—which had once been deeper than friendship and might in the future tend that way again, who knew?—was something he should have expressed more gratitude for. He had always valued the freedom he felt with me. Other people made him clam up and say nothing at all, but with me he felt open. He realized his unfiltered outpourings might sometimes have a repulsive effect, but he hoped I could see he had zero intention to hurt. It was not in his nature to tend toward violence of any kind; as I might remember from our school days, he'd always been the victim, never the perpetrator, of bullying. All the maltreatment he'd received at the hands of our schoolmates and teachers, coupled with the other knocks he'd taken in life, had turned him into a philosopher: rather than engaging directly with the systems around him, he was content to remain apart from them, on an island of sorts, observing, analyzing, theorizing, often in the form of verse and song. No doubt I considered him an idler, a good-for-nothing—how could I not, when I came from a family of white-collar professionals descended from the priestly class? While I'd have no trouble finding others who shared my opinion of him, he asked that I consider for a moment the hypocrisy of my own situation: I claimed to be a writer, but I was terrified of coming across as unproductive, which, were I indeed a serious writer, unafraid to spend hours each day dreaming and doodling, I inevitably would to my Brahmin parents and relatives, who, as I myself had once said, considered any pursuit of the arts frivolous. At some level, I must share their view: I must feel guilt at spending time writing, so therefore I had to keep up the appearance, to others and myself, that I was engaged in something respectable, a proper, worthwhile use of one's time. Hence my decision to be a teacher. He didn't want to judge me, he said in conclusion; the best thing for us would be to respect each other's decisions and stay in touch, the way old friends do.

I read this on my laptop, sitting on a bench outside the public library, where the Wi-Fi was strong enough for email. The library was down the street from the landlord's mother's house, which had no internet connection. I'd arrived from the airport that afternoon and, following the landlord's instructions, retrieved the key from under the cushion of the outdoor rocking chair, and let myself in. I smelled mildew and stale cigarette smoke. Daylight seeped through mesh curtains the color of bile. In the living room, a network of lace covers and doilies obscured, like giant spiderwebs, the couches and side tables encircling a faded rug. I toured the kitchen—crooked cabinets, stove caked with grease and dust—before ascending the listing staircase with my luggage. As I approached the second floor, a hairless old woman shuffled out of a room, dressed in a yellow bathrobe and slippers, a cane in one hand and an orange box of pills in the other. At the sight of me, she screamed and dropped the box.

I'd forgotten you were coming, she said, as I bent to gather the scattered pills. Jim, who used to rent your room—he was an elephant, and you're a mouse. I have to get used to a mouse in the house. She laughed throatily. You are a tiny thing, aren't you. Like a bird. I'll just think of you as a little bird nesting up there.

On my way up the remaining steps, I felt a sudden conviction that there would be no bay window, so when it appeared, with its view of the side garden as the landlord had promised, I felt enough relief to temper, for a few moments, my dismay at the peeling wallpaper, the narrow, hard-looking bed, and the moldy bathroom. There was no desk, only a spindle-backed reclining chair, which, no matter how I placed it, would not allow me to look out at the garden because the windowsill was too high. In order to type comfortably, I'd have to turn the chair sideways and rest my feet on the bed, a position that forced me to face not the window but the room itself. Eventually I put my computer in my backpack and headed out.

The bench by the library was sticky, the evening oppressive, my eyes watery from the sun, which had hovered in my peripheral vision for the entire flight across the Atlantic, a never-ending state of mid-day. I was glad, I wrote Ajit, that his health was better. I wished him well. Then I reminded him that I was starting a new life, on my own, away from home, and could no longer allow him to drag me down.

CHAPTER THREE

At orientation the next morning, we were a group of five—four new faculty members and Andy—gathered around a square made of long tables, the kind with collapsible legs. Each of us had before us a similar pile of materials accompanied by a printed slip of instructions. Andy brandished a digital kitchen timer from the tasseled leather pouch at his waist. Depict your journey to this place, he repeated, gesturing to the whiteboard behind him where he'd written the words in block letters. You have twenty minutes.

He jabbed a button, the timer beeped, and with an air of great purpose, he set upon his materials, grabbing sheets of newspaper and tearing them into strips. I was surprised that, as facilitator, he himself was participating in the activity. Beside me, Yuna, the new economics teacher, was folding her cardboard square in thirds. Earlier in the cafeteria, over breakfast, she'd said that she'd been in OPT status, too, her first year teaching, more than twenty years ago. Her parents, who lived in Seoul, had assumed she'd be going straight from undergraduate studies to a doctoral program. When they heard she wanted work experience after graduation, they then assumed, since she was an economics major, she'd get an internship at a bank or a hedge fund. So when she announced that she'd be teaching at an American high school instead, they asked if she'd been smoking pot or become depressed. Yuna's round face contorted with laughter as she said this, and the more she laughed the funnier she seemed to find it, until she was bent over and bracing herself against the table. Her laugh was buoyant and her hands were as small as a child's, with thick, strong-looking wrists. A single stripe of silver gleamed in her cropped black hair as she straightened up and shook her head.

Ten years ago, she continued, I took a break from teaching to open a bakery and art gallery with my then husband. I told my parents, See, I'm using my economics training to start a business. They told me I'd already brought enough shame on the family by not becoming an economist or lawyer or accountant, that at least teaching was something respectable, whereas any illiterate could start a bakery. My advice to you: don't bother even *trying* to make your parents happy. She brought her fist down on the table. Our plates of pancakes jumped, and the noise startled her. She unclenched her hand and studied her mug of tea. It's hard for them to imagine my life here, she said more softly. You know? It's like we're now the adults and they're the children—they can't understand our problems and challenges.

Six minutes left.

Andy's voice made me start. My materials lay before me untouched, with the exception of the roll of masking tape, from which I'd torn off a length that I now twisted absently between my fingers. I pasted it to my allotted sheet of cardboard, then peeled off another length and pasted it alongside. My head felt woolly from jet lag. If I kept my hands moving, I told myself, my depiction would take shape.

Time's up, Andy called with mock severity. Let's all present. Pete, can we start with you?

The new Spanish teacher and dorm parent stood briskly, flexing his knees and adjusting the belt around his khaki trousers. I grew up in Nashville, Tennessee, he began, holding his depiction against his chest. He'd covered the cardboard with newspaper and drawn a crude outline of the Americas, dots scattering the map. Never thought I'd be a Spanish teacher, but then in eighth grade I was lucky enough to join an exchange program and travel to Mexico City—he peered over the top of the map as his finger moved south—and live with a host family for three months. That's when my love affair with Spanish really began.

Andy interrupted. Do you have your sentence, Pete? To read aloud?

My sentence?

It's on the list of instructions. Write a one-sentence description of your piece and be prepared to read it aloud to the group.

Pete sniffed and rubbed his nose. I guess I missed that part, sorry. Do you want me to stop?

No, keep going. The point of the instructions was to make things clearer, not to overwhelm or confuse.

Pete's finger resumed its circling and tapping. Ecuador, Guatemala, Costa Rica: after his trip to Mexico City, he'd traveled to all these places as a member of a youth group charged with saving the rainforests. In college—his finger darted upward, to Maine, before swooping back down, well past the equator—he'd spent his junior year abroad, in Santiago, Chile. He stroked the western coast of South America, then tapped other dots nearby—countries he'd visited after graduation, hitchhiking across vast lengths of Peru, Argentina, and Brazil, picking up Portuguese along the way, often sleeping in hammocks or the backs of trucks, in a continuous state of marvel at how much the world contained and how little of it a single person could encounter in a lifetime. Which is why I became a teacher, he said, drawing his finger north again. I want to shake American kids out of the stupor this country lives in, this unquestioning assumption that the world revolves around us and our needs, our language, our way of life. I thought, Surely we'll be fighting fewer wars if more people have an actual sense of *what's out there*. He'd taught at an elite New England boarding school for the past twelve years because he believed it would give him an outsize influence, a moral influence, on the future CEOs and politicians of this country, but what he'd come to resist was his awareness of being owned by an institution whose endowment was invested in companies that helped fuel those same American wars he wanted to stop. So I decided to move to a smaller, quirkier sort of place, and here I am. He tapped the biggest dot on the map several times, then sat down.

Andy turned to Josephine, the new theater teacher. Jo, do you have your sentence ready?

Josephine rose, a purple-haired woman with shoulders so sloped and narrow that her ruffled, wide-necked dress seemed in danger of sliding to her elbows. It felt so good to use these again, she said to Andy, flexing her long, bony fingers. I've been reading too many scripts and really craving something tactile. I was thinking just last night, lying in bed, about my journey here, and I'm convinced I've come full circle. Been born again, for lack of a better term. The last time I felt this way, full of anticipation and some dread but an overall sense of good things to come, was when I was in kindergarten, about forty years ago.

Andy consulted his watch and let out his breath with a sigh. As Josephine kept talking, her voice began to sound like it was coming from far away, and the next thing I knew I was lifting my bent head, wondering where I was and feeling a crick in my neck.

So here I am, Josephine declared. As you see, I drew the car crash off to the side, unconnected to the rest of my life because I was quite literally cut off from the world before I returned. She clapped a hand to her chest and bowed, more a marionette than a person.

Andy stood, his sneakers squeaking against the floor as he held up his cardboard in one hand and a slip of notepaper in the other. His sentence conveyed that the zigzagging strips of newspaper depicted an erratic journey: the child of Harvard professors in Concord to Peace Corps volunteer in Africa to PhD candidate in Arizona to lab coordinator in Maryland to high school teacher here and his current positions as science-department chair and faculty liaison to the board of trustees.

He gave an emphatic nod and seemed about to sit down when he changed his mind and addressed us again. I was hoping that in addition to being an icebreaker, this activity would highlight some aspects of good pedagogy. Sometimes we get so carried away planning the details of an activity that we end up forgetting the whole point. When he was younger, his lesson notes used to go on for pages and pages because he feared that if he didn't script everything, he'd make a mistake and end up looking like a fool. The result of all that scripting was, predictably, that he made a fool of himself every time: he was stiff as a board, he looked more at his notes than at his students, and every time someone asked a question, he would regress back to the painfully shy teenager he'd once been. It was perhaps the reason he'd chosen to become a teacher: the chance to relive his adolescence with more control, and he suspected he wasn't the only one in this regard. He looked expectantly at us, anticipating agreement or resistance, and when nobody reacted, he gestured amiably to Yuna, who stood up and balanced on the palm of her hand a triangular pipe of cardboard wrapped with tendrils of newspaper. Instead of a sentence, she said, I have just three words. Displacement. Roots. Balance.

The group laughed. Andy seemed taken aback. You're sure you don't want to say anything more?

Quite sure, Yuna said. She looked at me and winked, as if the two of us knew something the others didn't.

■

Elena was waiting for me outside Punjabi Dhaba. It's like being back in high school, she said as we stood in line for mango lassis. Everybody's talking about their LSAT scores. And we each get a locker. They showed us today how to open and close them. But you— you actually *are* back in high school!

There was a strange moment, I told her, during faculty orientation that morning, when, just as I was about to introduce myself, I'd experienced a paralysis, as though the unbroken line I'd been traveling had suddenly vanished, both before and behind me. I was convinced I was levitating, that I'd fallen into a gap between two units of time. It reminded me of a question a professor had once asked from the lectern: If time is a series of discrete units, how do we understand the spaces between them?

Elena nodded slowly, her eyes closing while she sipped her lassi through the straw. She had an air of perpetual fatigue and boredom, as if holding herself upright took more energy than she cared to expend. In the room we'd shared our freshman year in college, she'd done all her studying in bed. Feet under the covers, hair swept up and pinned in a glamorous twist, her books and papers strewn around and caught in the swirls of her fleece blanket, she was an elegant shipwreck amid floating detritus. Something she'd always appreciated, she said now, opening her eyes, was how I could explain physics concepts in a way she could understand, or at least feel close to understanding. Her little sister was so different from her. Math and science were her thing. She wanted to be an aerospace engineer, which would be a big first in their artsy family, but Elena worried that the coming year might break Luisa's spirit. She was signed up to take Calculus III, a course known colloquially at the high school as Asian calculus because it was Asian students that dominated the roster. Luisa's friends thought she was nuts to be putting herself in with that group. In Elena's opinion, it was a course created specifically to cater to the demands of Asian parents who wouldn't stop complaining that their kids weren't being challenged enough in the regular courses—kids who must have been trained to recite their multiplication tables as soon as they could talk and who studied until three in the morning every day. Pandering, she called it. The school was pandering to a vocal minority, and as a result, kids like her sister, who, like all kids, deserved to live a balanced life, would be stressing themselves out to keep up.

We took our lassis to the park across the street and sat on a bench. Elena, in frayed denim shorts, stretched her legs out in front of her. She was deeply tan, I assumed from beach days in Valencia, where her family spent part of every summer in their ancestral villa. This is delicious, she said of the mango lassi. Did you have these all the time growing up?

Never, I said. I'd had mangoes, a wide variety of them every summer in India, and lassis, but never blended together.

You should start a trend in India then. I bet it would be popular.

I'd learned that day, I said, that there was a faculty-of-color group that met weekly at lunch. The term "of color" struck me as ridiculous. Only in America, it seemed to me, would people coin such labels as "person of color" and "legal alien."

Elena blinked at me. I've never thought of you as a person of color. I would never describe you that way. I mean, you're—you didn't grow up here, so it's fair to say you're a foreigner. Indian, specifically, since you're from India. I guess if you were a citizen, you'd be Indian American. If I were to describe your skin color, I'd say, gorgeous tan that I'm jealous of. But if you're supposed to be a person of color, then what am I? A person of no color? A non–person of color? Who the fuck cares, anyway? Are you all right? You look tired.

I was falling asleep from jet lag, I said, and needed to walk to keep awake. Elena suggested we go to Cambridgeport to see her new apartment. But can we take a quick look at your new place, since it's right here?

I said I still needed to get used to the old lady. She was, in essence, my housemate, and her snoring had woken me up several times in the night. It wasn't loud but of a frequency resonant with the furniture in my room. The previous evening, I'd gone down to get my dinner from the fridge—a boxed salad I'd picked up at the airport—and she detained me to ask if I'd been promised to someone, a question that stumped me. She'd had a nurse once, she went on, a young Indian woman who spoke English far less fluently than I did and whose skin was darker than mine, practically black. Pretty, in an exotic way, she said. She'd asked the nurse, Why does a beautiful girl like you not have a man? and in response the nurse allegedly giggled—she was a shy, sweet thing—and said her marriage had been arranged when she was three years old to a boy she'd never met who was waiting for her back in India. I said I wasn't promised to anyone and didn't personally know anyone who was. My response disappointed her. She adjusted her wig, which was blond, and thumped her stick on the kitchen floor. She had Prussian ancestry, some of noble blood: her great-great-great-grandparents had been in a similar situation to that of the Indian nurse and her betrothed, and so she'd always thought of

India as a place where old-world customs still flourished. They do, I told her, but they're getting less common. She then started to tell me about an Indian man she'd known growing up, a palm reader everyone called Guru, but I managed to excuse myself before she could elaborate.

I don't think I could live with her, Elena said. I'm such a brooder, I need my own space. If I had to be cordial and considerate the whole time I'm home, I'd go crazy. I'm envious of your rent, though. I'll be so deep in debt by the time I graduate, it's depressing to think about. She rolled her eyes and slumped further down on the bench. Her sloth-like air had always suggested to me that her opinions were more expressions of frustration than considered arguments. I think war stinks, she'd said when we were roommates, but I'm for what we're doing. After what they did to us. They're pure evil, they need to be wiped off the face of the Earth. Having slurped the last of her lassi through the straw, she now looked dejectedly at her cup. I don't believe it's possible anymore to live a moral life. I used to want to help battered women, orphaned kids; now I'll need to take a job at a law firm serving billionaires to have any chance at paying off my student loans. And once I get my debt under control, I'll be so accustomed to making that kind of money, I bet I'll just keep doing it. I get irritated reading about how when I buy a computer I'm supporting child labor and the illegal mining of rare-earth metals. Great, so what am I supposed to do? *Not* buy a computer? *Not* take flights anywhere? It's like what you said once, that you don't support American wars but your tax money goes toward them anyway. Anything, *anything* we do is evil. What's the right way to live? You tell me.

She pushed her empty cup into an overflowing trash bin, and we started to walk, her leading the way, me following, my unfinished drink in hand, trying to keep track of turns and street names so I'd be able to find my way home.

CHAPTER **FOUR**

On the crowded bus to Somerville, I was aware of how strong the parcel in my lap smelled. Coffee, curry leaves, tamarind—the frowns and twitching noses of my fellow passengers made me push the bag under my seat. On Highland Avenue, I got off at Walnut Street and walked downhill toward Union Square. The October wind from the valley below was colder than I'd anticipated; by the time I reached Gita's house, I was shivering.

They're predicting frost tonight, Gita said by way of greeting. She shut the door behind us, and at once I was enveloped by warmth and rich cooking smells. I handed her the parcel, given to me six weeks earlier in Bangalore by her mother. I hope everything is still fresh, I said, and she dismissed my concern with a flick of her hand. Past deliveries—half a dozen at least—of powders, preserves, and mixes were still sitting unopened in her freezer. She'd been trying for years to persuade her mother that there was no need to send anything, but the more she insisted, the more determined her mother seemed to maintain the flow of provisions. I should start warning our relatives and friends, Gita said as she led me into the kitchen. I should say, If you're planning a trip to America, you'll be on her hit list, so please make up some excuse—too much luggage already, no time—or she'll act like you run a courier service. Doesn't matter if you're headed to California or even Canada—she'll ask you to mail me the stuff.

That the traffic was now almost exclusively one way made these deliveries especially frustrating. Even ten years ago she used to get requests from back home to send jeans, gadgets, chocolates. Now she'd stopped asking what she could send or bring because the answer was always, We get everything here now. There was a certain glee in the way they said it, too, as if what her family really wanted to express was, America is not so great anymore; you no longer have things we want. It prompted in her something of a backlash: she'd taken to telling her mother she needed absolutely nothing, she was perfectly capable of roasting and grinding her own spices, thank you very much. But her mother would laugh and say, When I'm there, I see you pack a granola bar for lunch. Where do you have the time to cook?

She's bitter, Gita said, pulling the cork from a bottle of wine. We were standing by the stove, where a large, oblong Dutch oven exhaled steam from around the rim of its lid. I'm not surprised Amma feels such resentment. Married off at age nineteen, forbidden by her in-laws to continue her studies, and to now be watching her only daughter settled abroad, happily unmarried at forty-five, a tenured professor, financially independent—it would drive any woman in her sixties crazy, seeing what she might have been allowed to do had she been born twenty years later or simply said to my grandparents, Fuck off, I have my own plans. She chose not to be a renegade, and now all she can do is make these wild declarations of how America has turned me into a money-earning work machine; without her sending me puliyogare gojju and kootu podi, my diet will be nothing but granola bars, and I'll die a premature death from diabetes. Wine for you? Here's bread I made yesterday—rye with methi. And tomato thokku. Spread it on—it's like butter.

I bit into the bread, which was crusty and delicious, as Gita poured me a glass. Since our last meeting months ago, when I'd come up from Philadelphia for my interview at the school, her face and arms looked heavier—something I suspected her mother, along with so many of our mutual friends in India, wouldn't hesitate to comment on, for it was practically a form of greeting the way people back home remarked so easily to one another, women especially, about their looks: *Nice to see you—you've put on weight, no?*

Cheers, Gita said, to your first year teaching. She sipped the wine and grimaced. Give it a few minutes, she said and set her glass on the island, whose population of kitchen objects basked like museum pieces in the glow of the ceiling lights. The same recessed bulbs seemed to emphasize the dark creases under her eyes, which were large and lustrous, with long lashes and thick, unthreaded brows. As always, no makeup concealed the pockmarks littering her skin. Her jaw, despite its extra layer of flesh, was square, that solid, stubborn shape characteristic of her mother's side of the family. She sliced more bread, retrieved her glass, and swirled it at chest level, thrusting her chin forward as if facing down her teetotaling Brahmin relatives. It's opening up, she declared, having taken a long swallow, then gestured past the island toward a potted avocado tree and a small table set for two. Be sure you have a sanctuary somewhere, she said. A space you can retreat to. For me, it's over there.

It was essential, she'd found, to have a spot to sit that was out of sight of her computer and papers. Most nights, when she ate dinner by herself, she tried to do it at that little table, with music playing and a bit of candlelight, even when her impulse was to chow down a slice of pizza and get back to work. She remembered being shocked the first time she'd been told, by an American colleague, to take some time for herself each day. We never heard such things in India: take time for yourself, look after yourself, treat yourself—it would be considered the height of selfishness to say these things aloud. Never mind that Hinduism, as she'd argued in a recent article, was essentially a selfish religion: we had taken the principal of artha to an extreme, we'd made it acceptable for people to acquire infinite amounts of wealth with no obligation to share. She raised her glass to me. Teaching, as I'm sure you'll agree, is an altruistic profession. You're brave to be taking on American students. They're smooth talkers, they love the sound of their own voices, they always have opinions, but ask them to demonstrate actual knowledge and they'll yawn and shrug as if they don't understand why in hell they have to *learn* anything.

The wine had left a trail of warmth down my throat. I ate another slice of bread and felt a surge of well-being as I emptied my glass. I said that my experience of American students, so far at least—it had been five weeks since classes started—was somewhat different. Their sloppiness with multiplication tables and other basics did shock me, but I was struck by how ready they were to engage with questions beyond the scope of the syllabus. The other day, I'd asked my algebra class if they thought mathematics had been invented or discovered, and what followed was a discussion that left me somewhat in awe. Discovered, one student said, because mathematics is everywhere in nature and has been since long before humans came along. Snowflakes have fractal patterns in them, the Fibonacci numbers appear in pine cones and snails' shells, planetary orbits are conic sections. But wait, said another. It's not like those rules were written out somewhere, waiting to be discovered. Anything that's been written has been invented because language and writing are human inventions. A girl, the shiest student in my class, raised her hand. Is it like music then? she asked. Music is invented, too, but every single musical note existed before instruments—in bird songs, in animal calls, in thunder. Humans came along and organized the notes into scales and gave them names, so the writing of songs is invented, but the notes themselves were discovered. When I was fourteen, this sort of thinking would have been beyond me—all I could do, all I'd been trained to do, was memorize and regurgitate.

Gita had moved back to the stove to stir the enameled pot. When she turned around, she was frowning deeply, her wooden spoon raised like a gavel. It all feeds into this narcissism, she said. This emphasis on an individual's opinions instead of actual knowledge. I remember, when I was in high school in Calcutta, the teacher asked a question, and I responded by saying, Miss, I think— And she cut me off immediately. I am not interested in what you *think*, young lady, I'm interested in what you *know*, what you have *learned*. Give me *facts*.

Then we can talk about what you *think*. Your teenage students may be having a fun discussion in class, but what you're doing is a sort of enabling, offering them a soapbox, telling them, You don't have anything close to a mastery of mathematics, but we still want to hear your opinion on the subject. It's what makes this country so dangerous, this adolescent confidence, this readiness to pronounce judgment. What they need is a good rap on the knuckles to alert them to their presumptions.

The wine was heating my ears; I felt invigorated, ready to run up a hill. I told Gita that now that we had facts at our fingertips we didn't have to cram them into our heads as we did before. What we did with facts, or how we determined what was fact, was more important. Had we in India been encouraged to think beyond the formulas, beyond dates and events, beyond the endless verses and theorems and lists we'd had to "mug up," as we used to say, we might have been less jaded, as schoolkids, about the value of knowledge.

Gita scoffed as she refilled her wine. Infotainment, she said, swirling her glass again and glaring at its contents as if they reflected everything she disapproved of. Infotainment is what passes for teaching here. Sesame Street style, a colleague of mine put it. No tolerance for lectures. No slideshow without at least one cartoon or a movie. Kids say openly, in their evaluations, I learn more when I'm having fun! I want to say, Excuse me, I'm a scholar of religion, not a circus clown. But more and more I find myself behaving like an entertainer with the rest, cracking jokes at the podium, planning activities, deploying some new trick every ten minutes. I find it exhausting, I find it insulting, I'm astonished at myself for the level of spoon-feeding I provide. I suppose for you it will be easier. You seem more of a natural, more open to today's youth and their demands than I'll ever be capable of. I'm a researcher and writer, primarily; I teach only because it's part of the job.

I wanted to remind her that I, too, was a writer, an aspiring one, but since I'd made no progress on my novel in the past weeks, I hesitated. My book seemed to be retreating from me: the characters fading away, my sentences feeling increasingly dull and leaden, infused, it seemed, with the fatigue that gripped me whenever I sat down to write in my dingy room. Over the weekend, I'd emailed a professor I'd had a rapport with in college, telling her my woes, and she'd responded that I was experiencing nothing more than a temporary hiatus from my creative work, not unlike what so many career women go through when they have young children: all my best energy was being directed elsewhere, temporarily, toward establishing this new life, and she recommended I give myself time, at least a year, to settle. Her email increased my dejection: the prospect of making no headway for a full year seemed a colossal waste.

We sat down with our plates filled from the Dutch oven. A Persian-inspired dish, Gita said. She'd recently become obsessed with recipes from the Middle East, whose cuisines were both similar to and different from our own: a lot of the same spices and methods of cooking but with ingredients unique to their regions—sour cherries, dill, lima beans. She looked me up and down and asked if I'd been starving myself. There had been afternoons, I said with my mouth full, when I realized around four o'clock that I'd missed lunch, and I was too tired by the time I got home to do more than warm a can of soup. I was also reluctant to enter the kitchen when the landlord's mother was there, for as soon as the old lady saw me she'd start talking, and I always felt trapped by her ramblings.

You should take the leftovers home, Gita said. She settled back with her wine, looking almost glamorous with her cheeks faintly flushed and the folds of her chiffon scarf catching the light. If she had to live her life over again, she said, she might open her own restaurant. Indian-fusion cuisine. Traditional spices and cooking methods; local fruits, vegetables, and grains. Wild-rice pullao, kale kootu, cheese boards with tamarind jam and mango pickle. A few months ago, she'd thrown a dinner party with these items on the menu, and one of the guests, a woman she didn't know very well who'd come with a colleague, approached her to say that if she ever was serious about starting a restaurant, she need look no further for financial support. The woman was the founder of a hedge fund, a trustee at the university, and an enthusiastic vegetarian. No cuisine in the world, she made a point of saying, showcased the potential of grains and legumes better than Indian food. People in the West needed to have their eyes opened.

I was intrigued, Gita said. I assumed she'd been to India, and when she said she hadn't, I invited her to tag along with my research group to Trivandrum. She declined in a strange way—shook her head with a pained expression, and I thought, Well, she thinks she'll stick out in a group of college kids, most of them Indian— that's who takes my courses, after all, American-born desi kids yearning to connect with their roots. But that wasn't it. She told me, this blond woman whose ancestors must have arrived on the *Mayflower* for all I know, that she'd dreamed of India all her life, ever since she was a little girl, and so might not be able to bear the disappointment of reality. I assumed her vision of India was palaces and snake charmers and whatnot, so I told her, yes, it probably would, the sheer reality that is India, the heat and stench, would hit her in the face as soon as she stepped off the plane. She drew back as if I had just punched her. It gets me into trouble sometimes, my directness, my inability to sugarcoat things. Too harsh, some student will always say on their evaluation, too intimidating, she makes us feel disrespected, she makes us feel small. How these young ignoramuses can be allowed to evaluate their teachers is beyond me. Help yourself, there's plenty more.

I refilled my plate and resumed eating, this time more slowly. At some level, I told Gita, I understood this American woman's reluctance to go to India, since I myself still hadn't been to the Taj Mahal and harbored a certain reluctance to see that monument after so many years of having fantasized about it.

You should go see it soon, Gita said. It's discoloring, dissolving in pollution. Crumbling just like everything else in India. The last time I was in Mumbai, the flyovers struck me as indistinguishable from Roman aqueducts. I was sitting in a taxi, stalled in traffic, staring at those newly built concrete structures and feeling like I'd been tele-ported into the future and was visiting the ruins of an ancient city.

The hedge-fund manager's vision of India, she went on, developed from her encounters with an Indian man, in childhood. She grew up in what she called a boring suburb of Connecticut, which I imag-ine to have been some sort of enclave of the rich. Her father was an executive at a pharmaceutical giant and had an associate in Delhi, a Tamilian, who came every year or so to attend meetings with the board of directors. He would apparently arrive at their house with rice and urad dal in his suitcase. She described to me how he would soak them overnight in a mixing bowl, grind them up in a food pro-cessor, leave the batter to rise by the baseboard heaters, then make dosas on her mother's pancake griddle. She said they were her favor-ite food growing up, that having to wait those long months between his visits only made them more desirable. He looked like Gandhi, she claimed, a small man, bespectacled and bald, with a compelling sort of elegance that made him appear, when he declined the wines, liquors, and cigars offered to him by her father, not less but more sophisticated than other men she knew. I suspect he was the only educated, cultured brown person she encountered as a child. He told her how in Pondicherry he would step into the kitchen at dawn, when the parrots were up and singing, to find the plate he'd used to cover the vat of dosa batter the night before pushed off by its bubbling contents. And this became her image of India: an overflowing, effer-vescent, strong-smelling pot in a window beneath a great, rising sun, and colorful, noisy birds flying everywhere. Rice-lentil crepes, she called the dosas, a term she felt described them perfectly and that I should be sure to use on the menu. She was quite serious about fund-ing me. I want you to have everything you need, she kept saying. Find a location and I'll pay your rent. Pick the best equipment and send me the bill. Don't worry about the business side of things—I'll find you a manager. We'll be opening people's eyes, she gushed, we'll be edu-cating them. People have no idea you can make delicious crepes with-out eggs—they need to be educated. She kept saying that word as if it would convince a professor, when in fact the more she said it the more it turned me off. If instead she'd said, You spend so much of your life educating people, I'd like to fund this project for you to have some fun, to explore something that's just yours, knowing you'd find joy in sharing it, I might have responded differently.

I set down my fork. My head was spinning slightly, and I felt the waistband of my jeans digging into my taut, full belly. The desire to rest my head on the table and close my eyes became almost overwhelming. I heard Gita say she'd made shrikhand for dessert, and in my mind I saw the soft, whipped curds rise before me and spread across a blue sky like the clouds I'd watched as a child from the terrace of my parents' home, me leaning against the concrete water tank that always felt warm from the sun, as parrots shrieked in the mango trees all around.

CHAPTER FIVE

May, a student in my mechanics course, lingered after class. Her small face was downcast as she approached my desk. It was an expectation in China, she said, that any high school student who came to the United States beat their American classmates in mathematics and science. Considering how hard she had worked for this exam, the sacrifices she'd made—in the past she'd always conquered difficult classes like mine by sparing herself no effort—her score was unacceptable, so low by her standards that she may as well have failed.

I extended my hand for the graded exam booklet she was holding at her waist, and she averted her eyes as if repelled by the sight of her own answers, in tidy, elegant script, accompanied by my x's in red ink. Generally she was a demure sort, quiet, attentive, and inscrutable, more business executive than high school student in her tailored jackets, tight skirts, and thickly applied makeup now starting to run with tears. The crepe sleeves of her ivory blouse made a rasping sound as she dabbed her eyes with a tissue, and on her delicate wrist was a slender, gold-rimmed watch. If she'd been less primped, I might have told her that I understood the pressures of her family and culture, that I myself had grown up in a community of doctors, engineers, and accountants who'd convinced me that if I didn't get high marks in mathematics and science I was either lazy or stupid, and that in retrospect, it was the desire to prove I was neither of those things that had driven me to pursue physics in college; otherwise, I might have studied English.

Could she please have another chance? May asked. Her eyes gazed at me from within their circles of smeared mascara. If I were to give her another problem to solve, she would do so immediately, right now. She would show me she could do it.

I pointed out that if I did as she asked, I would be obliged to offer a retest to the entire class. Through a gush of sooty tears, she begged me to help her. She'd thought she'd learned everything there was to learn for the test; why she kept getting things wrong she couldn't understand.

With what I hoped was gentle firmness, I said she was relying too much on her intuition of how objects behave, an intuition that, as we'd discussed early in the course, reflected our tendency to think more like Aristotle than like Newton. I knew she was too worked up to listen properly, but not knowing what else to tell her, I recalled the example of riding a bus around a corner. Our intuition says there's a force pulling us outward when really the only force is the friction between our body and the seat, directed inward, trying to keep us from sliding off.

A fresh gush of tears. How can something like a seat on a bus *try*, she wailed, as if it were a living being, as if it had a goal in mind? When science teachers used words that gave desires to inanimate objects—atoms searching for electrons, objects wanting to stay on straight paths—she started imagining herself in the place of a cannonball about to be fired from a cliff and thinking, I have these equations in front of me describing all my possible paths, which one should I take? No matter how hard she tried, she always chose wrong. This was how she got cheated out of the grades she deserved.

What you need to do, I said, still trying to speak gently, is learn to tell the difference between equilibrium and nonequilibrium.

The look of anguish morphed into a glower. She ran her ivory sleeve over her cheek and backed away from me, legs tapering beneath her skirt to boots of a striated and glistening material like the hide of a snake. I don't know, she said, giving me a final sideways glance, her voice steadier now and full of loathing, why you became a teacher. It's obvious you don't like students and that we all don't like you.

■

When I returned to my office, the red light on my desk phone was blinking. 'Tis the season, a colleague had joked that morning. You send midterm reports to the parents and your phone starts ringing.

The recorded voice, a man's, rumbled in my ear like slow thunder. My son Noah has been steeped in physics all his life. All his life, you understand. Quarks, antimatter, the big bang—he was talking about these concepts when he was five years old. How he can do so poorly in a subject that's in his blood I find profoundly disturbing. He says you keep telling him he needs to master the basics, but I wonder if you even realize what a gifted child this is.

The answering machine beeped. Another voice, this one sharp and nasal, mispronounced my name. I'm calling to let you know I'm sick and tired of these reports about my kid needing to do a better job learning the material. It's the same story every year. If he won't listen to you, do you think he'll listen to his parents of all people? There's a reason I pay you folks, and that's to teach him what he needs to know to get into college—if he's not learning it, then you need to fix him, you understand?

I opened my computer. With numb fascination, I perused emails accusing me of intimidating the children whose education I'd been charged with. One parent accused me of destroying their daughter's love of mathematics, another of not understanding the damage that lack of positive feedback can do to a young person. It may just be Dora's perception that you're mean, the mother clarified, but you have to understand, her perception *is* her reality.

Andy was standing beside me. It would be good for us to talk, he said, and in a daze I followed him to his alcove. His desk was a sea of papers and spiral-bound notebooks bordered by a row of specimen jars. He steepled his fingers below his beard and contemplated me from behind the containers, whose contents appeared to be the divided innards of the same smallish animal: brain, lung, heart, kidneys, and entrails. He'd been in touch with the family of another student of mine, he said, from my physics class. The mother had written a letter six pages long and sent it as an email attachment. Perhaps it would be better to call it a rant. He'd thought about letting me read the whole thing—he did believe in transparency whenever possible—but the language was so raw, so disemboweling, especially in the sections that spoke directly about me that it would probably be better for him to summarize the concerns expressed. Before he did, though, did I want to tell my side of the story?

I looked behind me. A few of my colleagues were at their desks, working. Something in their air of absorption let me know that everybody was listening.

A complicated child, Andy said, was how he'd personally describe Dee. "Moody" was the adjective that came to mind when he remembered how she'd been in human anatomy—moodier than the average teenager, alternately enthusiastic and despairing. He remembered having to take her aside, when she was interrupting the lesson every few seconds, and try to calm her. Her parents would probably say—in fact they did say, in their letter—that if she came across as disruptive—"emotional" was the word they'd used—if she seemed emotional in class, it was because she was deeply invested in learning. He imagined that in a quantitative course like mine she'd need a fair amount of reassurance. Which is why my recent comment to her, which he assumed I hadn't meant cruelly, made her feel singled out and punished.

I asked Andy what exactly I'd been accused of saying.

They're claiming that when she asked for help solving a problem, you told her, or perhaps implied, that she was stupid.

All I recalled saying to Dee was that her work revealed a poor grasp of some basic mathematics.

Andy inhaled sharply, and I waited for him to voice his amazement at the parents' overreaction. I'm not sure, he said, if that's a useful thing for someone like Dee to hear.

I glanced once more over my shoulder, at my colleagues, with whom my interactions so far had been nothing but congenial, and wondered if beneath the friendliness they saw me the way my students and their parents seemed to see me: as cold, insensitive.

I observed, Andy went on, when I visited your class the other day, that Dee wasn't jumping up and down and interrupting the way she used to. I thought, Good, she's growing. I mentioned this to the parents—we talked on the phone this afternoon—they demanded I call them as soon as possible, and I was trying to defuse some of the tension there by saying I was impressed with how much calmer, how much more mature, Dee seemed. Well, that didn't land well. They said she was quiet because she felt muzzled—their word, not mine. Personally I thought, observing that class, that it was well managed, that your minimalist style can work well for many students. I could see by the way you were talking that you would not tolerate interruption. You didn't stop at any point to check that everybody was still following. You just went on, step after step after step. I was quite engrossed, I was carried along by the eloquence of your explanations, wishing I could go back and relive my own physics experience. But for an anxious kid like Dee to feel comfortable, you'd probably need to go out of your way to dispel her fears that she's no good at math.

I suppressed the urge to ask if I should have told Dee her algebra was correct when it was not.

Is there anything else, Andy asked, that you think I should know?

Dee wasn't in class today, I said.

That's because I switched her to Roland's section. It seemed from the parents' letter that the situation had gotten toxic.

That last word echoed in my ears as I returned to my desk and picked up the ringing phone.

I just wanted to let you know, the voice, a woman's this time, said. Sally won't be in class tomorrow. She fell during hockey practice and sustained a minor concussion. Nothing terribly serious, but I'd like to keep her under observation. Sally loves your class, by the way.

I cleared my throat and expressed thanks.

Yes, she's a motivated one. Not like my son, who never saw the point of school. I'm always amazed by how different my two are. David I was always having to hound, Sally I need to pry from her books or she'll stay up through the night studying. She loves a challenge, as I'm sure you've noticed. She keeps telling me I should meet you on parents' night. Mom, she says, you've got to meet my teacher—she's this drop-dead gorgeous woman who tells the most awesome stories and can juggle books like a circus clown.

I rubbed my head, which was throbbing. I think you're confusing me with someone else.

You know, you're right. Remind me of your name again?

The blinking light on the machine indicated another message. A male voice, gruff and slightly nervous, wished me good afternoon. I appreciate you letting me know, ma'am. I'm very disappointed in my boy. He knows better. He can *do* better. He told me at the start of the year that he was going to stop fooling around, that he was going to do his homework every day and be responsible, but you know what? This just shows that he ain't being responsible and I'm going to have to crack down on him. He's on scholarship, as you know, and that scholarship won't last unless he gets his grades up. So thank you, ma'am, for your timely notice, and I hope you'll see a change in my boy.

I put the receiver back on its cradle and tried to prepare for the next day's classes, but when it was time to gather my things and leave, I'd written no more than a single line of notes. The whir of a vacuum cleaner sounded in the hallway outside, accompanied by voices speaking Portuguese. They belonged to the janitors, a man and a woman I'd seen before and assumed were a couple, the way they laughed, talked, and moved through the empty classrooms with their mops and dusters, always side by side like dance partners. I'd waved to them more than once on the many evenings I'd stayed late; today the woman called out to me as I passed them. She had round, radiant cheeks and a musical voice. Always you stay late, she said, always you're working too much. The man added, You from where? India? and smiled kindly as I nodded and backed away. They were both dressed in T-shirts and soft slippers, as if whatever warmth they needed they drew from their companionship. My body, in its casings of sweater and coat, felt like it was being turned to stone as I set out in the cold wind for home.

CHAPTER SIX

At lunch the next day, Olga, a mathematics teacher, studied me from across our shared table. Let me deduce, she said, pointing at my forehead with a celery stick. I predict that parents whose kids did not get high grades are saying problem is you. Yes?

We were sitting by an open window. Outside, men with leaf blowers were circling the quadrangle, pushing dead leaves that, reanimated by the noisy gusts of air, leaped like flying fish.

Same thing happened to me my first year, Olga said. Parent call, say, Why you give my daughter C? I think, I beg your pardon, *give*? I'm Santa Claus, my job is to *give*? Your daughter *earn* C—why? Because she has not demonstrated strong understanding of mathematics. Student come to me, she say, I worked so hard, why did you give me C? I say same thing. Because you did not demonstrate strong understanding of mathematics. And then everybody here say, Oh, Olga, you're bad, you're mean, you have to be encouraging, you have to be positive. They think I'm dictator because I come from Soviet Union, but in my Russian head I'm just telling truth. Truth, fact, logic—in America people don't want these things. In America, everybody wanting opinion. Even in math department, end-of-year evaluation form has, Agree or disagree: teacher is open to differences of opinion. What opinion? Is *math*! She sank her teeth into the celery stick, a small-boned woman with an upturned nose and orange hair, whom I'd overheard students describe as "dorky," a term I imagined had something to do with her loud voice and equally loud outfits: frilly, sequined dresses in mismatched colors, sleek fur coats, and laced boots with outrageous heels.

Stephanie slid into the seat beside me and placed a hand on my arm. Oh my god, are you okay? Andy said it was rough, that you might need moral support. How are you feeling?

There was something I didn't understand, I said. How as a teacher was I supposed to help any student learn material they should have learned a long time ago without pointing out the lapse?

Olga fanned herself with a crimson boa. She used to get angry, she said, at American students' ignorance, but these days it made her laugh. I say to kids, Ha ha, time for game: let's pretend we're in kindergarten, okay?

Stephanie, her hand still on my arm, leaned closer to me. Would you be comfortable telling us a bit more?

The reason Dee was stuck, as I'd told her, was that she didn't seem to know how to add fractions, something she should have learned in middle school.

Stephanie released me, flinching. That's a bit harsh. I mean, she could have had a bad teacher in middle school.

I hadn't said it harshly at all; I'd simply stated it as a fact. When I was in school, if a teacher let me know I was displaying ignorance about something I should have learned earlier, I'd think, Oh no, I'm making a fool of myself—and go home to study.

Stephanie's eyes widened behind her pink spectacles. That's so *interesting*, she said. That's *fascinating*. She slapped the table triumphantly. The previous year, at a faculty meeting, a diversity consultant had handed out an article about the differences between Eastern and Western models of learning, models based on patterns of conversation between people in various languages. In Western cultures, according to the author, the task of understanding fell to the speaker, whereas in the East, it was the listener's responsibility. So, Stephanie said, touching my arm again, in *your* culture, anything a student is taught in an earlier class is going to be their responsibility to learn or relearn. Whereas here, an American kid will expect you to reteach them everything, again and again. It just goes through them like a laxative. Well, what do you expect? We're the biggest consumers, the biggest warmongers, the biggest polluters—responsibility is not really our thing. Right, Olga?

Olga wagged a finger at me. Dee is stupid. I'm just telling you truth, that girl is stupid. But in this school, we are not allowed to say anybody is stupid. So, what do you do? You say something that is not truth, also not lie. You tell Dee, My dear, I see you are struggling. It is most useful word I've learned in English language—struggling. I used to think, struggling means *struggling*: my grandparents, how they ate wallpaper and rats during the war; my parents, how they raised us in Soviet times. These American kids, struggling? But now, every time I want to tell student, You're dumb, you're lazy, you should go back to kindergarten, I remind myself, No, no, Olga, this is not good, you will get only yourself into trouble. So I take deep breath and I tell kid, You're *struggling*. Then nobody has any problem.

I disagree, Olga, Stephanie said solemnly. I disagree that Dee is stupid. I think she's a complicated child from a complicated family. She has some issues that require holistic responses. Calling her stupid I don't think is helpful.

Ah, you Americans, Olga said cheerfully, you want complicated solution when problem is simple. And when there is no problem at all, you want to *make* problem so you can have complicated, expensive solution. She got to her feet and buttoned her extravagant coat. I have meeting with mother who thinks her son is wunderkind. I'm going to tell her, Yes, yes, absolutely, Parker is wunderkind. He's struggling to submit his homework on time, struggling to study, struggling to take responsibility—but he's wunderkind, I agree, and his mother will say, Thank you so much for understanding, and that will be end of meeting.

Communist background, Stephanie whispered as Olga strutted away. Anyhow, I came to tell you I think Andy went about it all wrong.

She squeezed my arm again the way I'd seen her do with distraught students, sitting alongside them and leaning into their woes, something I knew I could never do without paralyzing self-consciousness. Andy, she said, should have had a meeting with the two of you, you and Dee. He should have told Dee, Look, you have a fantastic teacher here, let's have a *conversation* about why the class isn't working well for you. Instead what he did was throw you under the bus. He shies away from conflict, Andy does. He thought he was doing you a favor and at the same time making the parents happy by taking Dee out of your class. He did a similar thing my first year. A student of mine felt entitled to go to him with this long list of reasons I never should have been hired. And Andy, being who he is, listened seriously and said, It sounds like the class isn't working for you, do you want to switch out? I was disturbed when it happened, as I'm sure you are now. I kept worrying that if my supervisor thought I couldn't handle this kid, then what did that say about me as a teacher? You need to eat something. Let me get you a sandwich.

I gazed out the window at the herders with their jet packs still pacing back and forth as they rounded up the last of the autumn leaves. A breeze, unnaturally warm and full of dust and gasoline fumes, prickled my eyes. I turned away to find Marie, an English teacher, sitting across from me in Olga's vacated chair. We were barely acquainted; now she greeted me with a solemn nod, her head, wrapped in a colorful cloth, bent low like a heavy flower on a thin stem. I've been meaning to tell you, she murmured, how impressed I was by the way you handled my advisee. He respects you because you don't bullshit him. You tell him what he needs to hear, which is that he doesn't know what he needs to know. You said if he spent half as much time on his math homework as he does skateboarding, he wouldn't be failing— no one here has ever said that to him before.

These words heartened me a little. I'd received a voice message from the boy's father, I said, and found him to be refreshingly sensible—the rare parent who responded not with hostility to my notification that their child was doing poorly but with appreciation and seriousness, the way an Indian parent, my own parents, would have reacted had a teacher of mine sent them a note saying I needed to work up.

Marie's eyes, with their bell-like lids, moved cautiously left and right. Honestly, she said, I don't think our school is the right place for him. It's not the right place for most Black kids on scholarship. The main thing they learn is how to charm their white teachers. It's not a nonessential skill, white schmoozing, as you and I both know, but it kind of breaks my heart to think that his parents want him to learn the things his middle school failed to teach him, like how to write proper sentences and do basic math, and here my colleagues are saying they don't want to break his spirit by giving him grammar drills, how in love they are with him, what a riot he is, how quick witted and fun. Such a great kid, there's no way I can give him an F—that's what they'll say—and he knows it, which is how he's gotten so far without flunking out. You and I, we don't let him get away with that crap, but I seriously wonder how much difference it'll make in the end.

The main reason, I said, leaning in, I felt drawn to a school like this was its promise of a kinder, more open-minded environment than the one I'd grown up in, but now I sometimes missed the harshness of the old ways. I was hard on her advisee because once I started speaking to him I sensed he'd understand me the way an Indian kid would. And he seemed to listen, he didn't interrupt me—this boy about twice my size, who could have picked me up with one hand—he looked at the floor between his feet, and when I finished, he mumbled something like, Okay, I get it, I'll do better, and I felt for the first time that my words as a teacher may have had an important effect.

You need to be careful, Marie said. I hear the investment in your voice, the caring. You'll do what I do, give him hours and hours of one-on-one time, bleed yourself dry, and believe me, he'll run you into the ground, the school will, if we're not careful.

I recoiled. I did not want to be run into the ground, I almost said aloud.

I know, Marie said, watching my expression. It's just what we do. Why do we feel the need to keep giving and giving, us brown and

Black women in particular? Just *living* in this world is stressful enough, why do we take it upon ourselves to do so much that we're about to split at the seams, and feel even so that there's more to do, it's our job to do it? She wrapped her long hands around a coffee cup. Of her fifteen years teaching, this one had started off the hardest. It was the raku class that did it, the first class she'd ever taught in a discipline other than English. It had taken her years to persuade the art department—the whitest department at the school, as I'd no doubt noticed—that she was qualified to teach kids how to use a potter's wheel and kiln. She'd been throwing pots since she was a teenager; every summer she spent weeks in a studio making mugs and bowls; a private gallery in Cambridge displayed and sold her pieces. Still, the chair kept finding reasons not to let her in. Why she'd kept asking she wasn't sure—partly it was her desire to be known beyond her established roles: teacher, adviser, athletics coach; partly it was to test whether the prejudice against her was real. For seven years she'd kept up her appeals, and when this year the chair finally said yes, she'd felt not gratitude but resentment so deep she almost changed her mind and told him, Thanks but no thanks. In retrospect, she should have said just that; instead, she'd gone and shared with the school, her place of labor and income, what used to be a private joy, and as a result the joy was contaminated.

Stephanie reappeared with a peanut butter sandwich. Ran into Lila, she muttered, setting the food before me. She wants you to go to her office right now. Some visa thing. Turning to Marie, she went on: Did you hear Lila's comment today at breakfast? About how she wishes all the Black students wouldn't sit at the same table?

I took my plate downstairs to the business office. Oh, there you are, honey, Lila said. Here's our petition for your H-1B. She tapped a sheaf of papers with the capped end of her pen, the gems on her fingers glinting. The lawyers want to file next week at the latest. I spoke to them this morning, and they said the earlier and the more thorough the application, the better. It's a good thing we're a nonprofit, honey, and exempt from the visa allocations. As you probably know, the quota for tech workers from India fills up very quickly every year because there are so many of you applying. Maybe you have a friend in the mix there?

The fluorescent ceiling bulbs gave her skin a greenish tint and shone straight through her thinning hair, exposing the scalp underneath. I guess that's a silly question, honey, when there are a billion of you. But you never know—my husband and I were traveling in Greece some years ago and ran into friends of ours we hadn't seen in a decade. What are the chances? Anyway, look it over today if you can. You'll see that we have to argue you were hired because it would have been difficult for us to find an American with the same qualifications. You'll also need to make an appointment at an American consulate abroad as soon as possible. Are you going home for winter break?

I hadn't planned to, I said, as airline tickets were particularly expensive in December.

Then in April?

I'd been hoping not to have to travel home until the following summer. My OPT status was valid until July, so could I not go to India in June and obtain my new visa then?

Her jowls shook in disapproval. That might be cutting it too fine. The lawyer seems to think we should get this petition in as soon as possible. It never used to be like this, believe me. I've watched the applications to hire foreign nationals grow fatter and more expensive. Not for you, but for us. It's the employer who pays. The government can't make it too easy for people to come here can it? We're overrun already. We want real salt-of-the-earth people, decent, hardworking folks that are worth every penny. If they were all like you, we'd have no problems, honey, but it's not that way, is it now?

CHAPTER SEVEN

The landlord would come by at two, he said, to inspect my malfunctioning radiator and take me somewhere nice for tea. He couldn't believe it was November already; he'd been meaning to look me up. I wondered how to dress, whether "somewhere nice" meant a casual or formal sort of place. In the end I put on my best jeans—a black pair from India—and a collared white shirt.

You waitressing? he asked when we met downstairs. He held a bottle of wine in one hand and a metal toolbox in the other. Without his spectacles he looked less professorial, his blue eyes, as they surveyed me, bright with something like mischief, his graying hair fashionably uncombed. He wore a purple tie that traced the arc of his belly. His corduroy jacket, which I remembered from our meeting in May, was tight around the shoulders, as if he were raring to burst out of it. White looks great on you, he said. Reminds me I need to get my tux dry-cleaned. Let me give this to my mother—he gestured with the bottle. Now and then I like to buy her a decent wine, something other than the crap she's pickled in.

He strode to the kitchen. Over the sounds of the TV set, I heard his chipper greeting and the old woman's raspy response. I wondered if she was complaining about me. An encounter with her daughter, Valerie, a few days earlier had left me shaken and bewildered: I'd returned from work and was going up to the third floor when loud, swift footsteps sounded from the landing below. A stocky woman in a belted cardigan was looking up at me, hands planted on her hips, an oily pink scowl for a mouth. You're sharing a house with my ninety-three-year-old mother. Didn't your parents teach you manners? That when there's a senior citizen around, you need to check on them, offer to get them groceries, bring in the mail? I live all the way in Melrose, I can't visit every day. I was assuming my brother kept an eye on her, but no, he's off to the Cape whenever he pleases. Her voice broke. She glared at me and wiped her eyes with the backs of her wrists.

Later that same evening my radiator began to clang and hiss, flooding the room with heat and a sharp metallic odor. I spun the wheel-like handle on the pipe to no avail. In my dreams, the noises became angry shouts. Faces peered down at me from a great height, their features twisted in disgust as I, a little creature on the floor, darted frantically about for an escape.

The landlord joined me upstairs and knelt beside the wheezing radiator. Phew, he said, it's like Death Valley in here.

Until last week, I told him, the heat rising from the lower floors was enough to keep the room warm. Of course, he said, retrieving a wrench from his toolbox and fitting it to the pipe, Ma likes to set the thermostat to the temperature of the sun. His hands, large and hairy with chapped knuckles, shuddered from the effort of tightening the valve. When the hissing stopped, he gave a loud grunt and got to his feet, staggering a little, wrench still in hand, tie askew, his long hair spilling over his ruddy face. Boiler's going on thirty years, he said. It's ancient, this whole system. No good replacing bits of it when all that makes sense is a proper gut job. We'll have to rip everything out—floors, pipes, electrical—after she leaves the house, which, as she reminded me just now, she'll be doing when we carry her out feetfirst.

He straightened his tie and looked around. The sunlight coming through the bay window lit up the mismatched and crooked surfaces, which I tried to keep neat by putting away as many of my things as would fit into the tiny closet and my desk drawers. I used an open bookcase to store my underwear in a basket, and I felt embarrassed now that this was visible. But the landlord seemed focused on a spot above my bed. This used to be his room, he said, until he was sixteen, when he moved to his father's house in Lexington. It was around the time he became serious about school—before then, he was out all the time with his friends smoking weed. Then once he decided to pay attention to his studies, he quickly realized it was impossible to concentrate in this space. Living with his mother and sister was like sharing a house with an active volcano: daily, deafening eruptions that could last for hours and into the night. He felt the floorboards vibrate from all the foot stamping and slamming of doors, the shouting, cursing, and name calling. All mothers and daughters, he imagined, went through phases of mutual hostility but few as extreme as what he'd had to witness.

I thought about how, when I was sixteen, I had, for the first time in my life, after an argument with my parents, slammed a door in frustration, an act my mother must have found deeply repugnant, for in the hours and days that followed she left no room for doubt, through her chiding sneers, and colder than usual attitude, that she considered me unworthy of her love, and when days later she emerged from that anger, ready to speak normally to me again, I relished giving her the silent treatment in return. Certainly, I told the landlord, I'd harbored hostile feelings toward my parents as a teenager, but since I wasn't permitted to scream or curse, I'd cry tears of fury into my pillow and fantasize about running away.

And run away you did, he said. You ran all the way here. I could have done with less fighting in the house. I'm surprised the neighbors never called the police. Even now, standing here, I can feel my old anticipation of yelling and screaming from downstairs. It's bred in me a lifelong appreciation for quiet. As he loosened his tie and started unbuttoning his collar, I backed away, but then he plunged his hand in his shirt, pulled out a strand of prayer beads and held them close to his face as if to reassure himself they were still intact. He stretched them out to give me a better look and slowly pronounced an Indian name. He'd spent a month in isolation at that ashram, he said, and the experience had blown his mind higher than any drug had managed to do. It helped him discover a deep silence within himself, which now, more than three decades later, he could still tap into by sitting in a chair, closing his eyes, and chanting "aum." Needless to say, his sister thought he was a freak.

The other day, I said, she'd seemed worried about their mother being here alone.

Oh, don't judge Val too harshly, he said as he dropped the beads back into his shirt and rebuttoned his collar. She's without doubt the unhappiest person I know. It gives me no joy at all to say this, but it's a fact: people like her are determined to stay unhappy. Let's get going. He took the stairs at a trot, whistling, one hand in his trouser pockets, the other swinging his toolbox. His mother was shuffling through the foyer as we descended; he bounded up and wrapped her in a squeeze. Well, Ma, we're heading out for some fresh air.

The old woman teetered briefly from the force of his hug and grasped the sleeve of his jacket to steady herself. For the first time, I saw a resemblance to the landlord and his sister—the same aquiline nose, a hardness about the mouth. She blinked at me as I came closer, then raised a gnarled, admonishing finger. When I was a little girl, she said, there was this Indian man we called Guru who came to dinner once a month. Beautiful dark eyes and brown skin like yours—here she reached out and stroked my hand. Guru was a vegetarian, so he couldn't eat very much of what my mother cooked. He was also a fortune teller. He told my mother in 1931 that she was about to experience a great sorrow, and sure enough, she suffered a miscarriage a few months later. He predicted many other things, too, some of which did happen. He certainly sounded like he believed it all. Anyway, you remind me of Guru.

Her withered face was smiling. It was hard to imagine her in a heated argument, let alone fight, with her daughter—but then my own mother was often described as mild mannered, pleasant, even kind by friends and acquaintances.

Just because she's from India, Ma, the landlord said loudly, doesn't mean she has any connection to Guru. There are a billion people in India. You know that, right? He turned to me and without lowering his voice said, She grew up on a farm in Iowa. It was—is—shall we say, a homogenous sort of place.

Outside, as I buttoned my coat, he picked up a glossy campaign flyer that had been left on the steps and said, Given that I already voted for him and he won, I think we can get rid of this, don't you?

The election had been the dominant subject lately at his discussion group. He'd assumed everyone would be happy about the state's first Black governor, but there was a fair bit of angst. What his election really showed, someone said, was that for a Black man to get elected, he needed to act white. No anger, no outrage, no making white people feel bad for the sins of their forefathers. The landlord wanted to say, If you're nothing but angry and resentful, you're not going to have much of a shot as a politician, doesn't matter who you are—but he hesitated. One had to be careful what one said aloud at these meetings. The young members, especially, were quick to label. He'd overheard a woman refer to him and two other white guys in the group as "the Three Stooges"—as if the three of them were simpatico simply because they were white and guys. He remembered listening to his elders discuss politics and sometimes thinking, You old farts need to just shut up and get out of our way—perhaps he needed to accept that it was his turn now to be dismissed.

Where should we get tea? Do you have time for a ride?

I walked with him to his car, an orange convertible with the top down. I expected the wind to be cold, but as we sped down Cambridge Street, the sun compensated, streaming straight into my face and at times blinding me. The landlord took a back road with many sharp turns and rolling hills, past large houses and stretches of unbroken woods. He was an aggressive driver who liked to gain on a car, hover close behind it, and then, with a roar of his engine, swerve into the oncoming lane and race ahead. The wind blew his long hair and lifted it over his ear, which I observed to be very large, as if an ear from a much bigger head had mistakenly gotten affixed to his. While we waited at an intersection for the light to change, I was aware of people staring from neighboring vehicles, whether at the convertible or the pair of us in it, I couldn't tell. There was a moment when the landlord's hand groped the space between us as if he were reaching for my hand, but then his fingers closed on a stick of chewing gum propped in the cup holder. I slid my palms under my thighs. He pointed out an institutional-looking brick building ahead. It was a highly reputable nursing home for the elderly, he said, the sort of place his mother might need to be moved to if her health deteriorated. And look what's right across the street, he added with a chuckle as we passed a funeral home, its pair of hearses parked beneath a black awning.

In Concord, the trees lining Main Street were denuded. Crisp, shriveled leaves skittered along the curbs; campaign signs still dotted the lawns. The breeze was mild, the sun still bright, and as we got out of the car and joined the throngs of people—mostly tourists—on the sidewalk, I felt my nervousness subside. The landlord gestured to an arrow pointing to Orchard House and said he'd never been there himself—had I? Yes, I said—after my interview last spring, I'd taken the commuter rail here and reached it ten minutes before closing time. The woman at the reception desk was reluctant to let me in, but when I told her that I was returning to Philadelphia that same night and had no idea when or if I'd be able to make another trip, that I'd read *Little Women* many times as a child in India and would find it very meaningful to tour the author's house, she relented and showed me around herself. I'd brought along my camera and took pictures to send to a friend of mine in Bangalore, a girl I'd grown up with, who, like me, had been obsessed with the book. Together we'd gone through a phase of acting out chapters and scenes. Setting up was my favorite part of the exercise: we would go up to the terrace and hang bedsheets over the clotheslines to build our version of Orchard House. Once the walls and ceiling were in place and we took shelter inside from the blazing sun—which in our imaginings became a raging New England snowstorm—I quickly became resentful, for my friend always wanted to be Jo, the character I also wanted to be. My friend couldn't play anyone else in the book, she claimed, because she *was* Jo—rebellious, ambitious, and spirited. When I pointed out that of the two of us, I was the writer, like Jo, she countered that my personality was more like Meg's, quiet and virtuous, which infuriated me, for I found Meg boring. All these years later, my friend, after completing an engineering degree, had been hired by a tech start-up for a salary that afforded her a penthouse apartment in Bangalore and a chauffeur-driven car. She wrote back that the house looked rather drab, which made me tempted to retort that she'd turned from Jo into Amy, ready to turn up her nose at anything that wasn't posh.

The landlord ushered me into a bustling café. It had always impressed him, he said, during his travels in India and Southeast Asia how knowledgeable people were about American politics, books, pop music, movie stars; the ubiquity of English, how easy that made it to get around. In Jakarta he'd found a nightclub with an astonishing repertoire of American country music; his host family in Goa had been the most die-hard Michael Jackson fans he'd ever met and made him wish he knew half as much about their country as they did about his; he felt it a great pity that Americans were so insular and ignorant—he wished it weren't so, but, as he'd pointed out at a recent discussion-group meeting and ruffled some feathers as a result, it must reflect *something* good about America if people who lived here had no desire to leave and people outside wanted to be allowed in. Power, someone in the group had shouted, it's all about power, the way America forces itself on the rest of the world, and he realized his statement had been misinterpreted. He tried to clarify that he was in no way referring to the American government or military, but it was too late—his companions were already shaking their heads as if he'd just declared an intent to murder. He wondered sometimes why he went to these meetings when he was attacked for simply expressing an opinion; he supposed it was his fundamental curiosity about people—the same curiosity that made him know all the names of his tenants and where they were from and what they did—that kept him returning.

As we stood in line to order, he asked how my time at the school was going. I answered that there was a great deal about America and Americans that I hadn't known prior to starting the job. His eyes widened, and he asked me to elaborate. When I mentioned the hostile reactions from students and parents to my teaching, he nodded with something like resignation. He recognized what I was describing, he said; what I needed to understand was that in America we had capitalism. Once you accepted that, then it was easy to see how education was less an entitlement and more a service, which made the kids more clients than students and the goal client satisfaction. In a retail sense, students were not so much customers as they were commodities: products to be packaged so they'd catch the eye of a college admissions officer and be picked off the shelf. Listening to his friends' anxiety-ridden stories about their kids' résumés and college applications always made him relieved not to have children of his own.

We sat by a glass fireplace where pale, bluish flames floated over a neat arrangement of fake logs. The landlord asked me what I wrote about. He knew Indian women writers were in vogue these days— he'd read a couple of them himself. He suspected it must be quite easy to write stories set in India. All you had to do was stand at a street corner, and you'd be at the center of all kinds of drama. He'd kept a notebook when he was in Delhi. He remembered thinking, sitting at a tea stall near his hotel, that if he were just to document everything around him for a week, he'd have a book. He wouldn't need to make up anything—the craziest stuff happened all around you all the time, spontaneously. The characters that showed up—human, animal, and everything in between, the things they did, the way that world accommodated all of it, those buses he'd seen so filled with passengers they seemed ready to explode, how they still rolled along, how everything rolled along. A miracle, he'd said to himself many times a day when he was there, a sheer miracle. You know what I mean, of course, he said, you grew up there. And you've been here long enough to know the contrast between your world, which I assume is the world of your stories, and the all-too-common setting for American literature: cold, colorless suburbs full of depressed, alcoholic people.

Sitting in a dentist's office the other day, he'd read a story in a magazine, a fictional story by a Filipino writer. A young woman, the author's alter ego undoubtedly, who is studying at an American university, goes home to her family in Manila and walks around feeling disconnected. He couldn't say he found it satisfying because a good chunk of it, close to half, in fact, was set in America—in Boston, actually. He found himself skimming over those sections—he knew, after all, what the Common and the Charles were. He wanted to read about the Philippines because that was a world new to him. He kept thinking, If this woman, the writer, was Filipino, and wanted her work read in America, wouldn't she do better to write about her own country? Give American readers a window onto a different world? But maybe she had another audience in mind—maybe she thought she was introducing Filipino readers to America. It must be a bit of a tightrope walk, he imagined, for writers like her and me to decide where we belonged. He knew something about living in two worlds. He was getting married next week to his boyfriend of many years. If my dad were still alive, he said, I might have invited him to the ceremony. But Ma has no idea it's happening. She still doesn't believe I'm gay. He has low sex drive is all: that's what she tells her friends.

He chuckled and bit into the roast-beef sandwich that had just been set in front of him. I sipped on a mulled apple cider, feeling relieved. Congratulations, I said.

He raised his coffee cup and gestured for me to help myself to an enormous cookie he'd bought at the bar. Only recently had he reacquainted himself with oatmeal raisin, which he'd developed an aversion to as a kid. At summer camp one year, his counselor, a drill sergeant of sorts, had singled him out as a troublemaker. We were supposed to eat breakfast at six in the morning. I wasn't hungry, so I stuffed this packet of instant oats into my pocket and showed him my empty bowl. Did you eat your oatmeal? he asked, like he wanted me to lie. Once we were on the lake canoeing and his back was turned, I opened the packet and dumped the oats into the water. I thought they would sink, but no, they radiated out across the surface in front of everyone. God, did he have it in for me after that. People like you, he yelled over and over, people like you are what's wrong with the world. You're double-faced. You can't be trusted. At the time I thought the guy was crazy. Who freaks out like that over a pack of oats? Now, of course, I know what he was objecting to—he was aware I was gay well before I knew it myself, the way pedophile priests must have an intuition for these things.

One of the details that struck him about India was how freely boys and men walked around hand in hand, something you almost never saw here. Amazing, he said, how uptight we Americans can be.

In my experience, I said, homophobia was very much alive in India: I remembered a classmate of mine, a boy, being teased mercilessly for his high voice and hip-swaying walk. He was once forced to kneel beside a girl and propose marriage to her. Though I didn't participate directly in the taunting, I remembered laughing along with others, a fact I was now ashamed of.

As I spoke, the setting sun edged into full view, past the half-drawn shade beside us. The landlord nodded, raising a hand to shield his face from the light. It's the air we breathe. When anyone in his discussion group confessed to having held mistaken beliefs, someone would remind them that it was the air we breathed.

I couldn't see the landlord's expression, so I wasn't sure if he meant to soften the implication of my childhood prejudice, or if he didn't believe the adage and thought my regret was insufficient. By the time the sun dipped out of sight, he was standing and brushing the cookie crumbs from his clothes. Let's get you back home, he said briskly. I'm guessing you have work to do.

CHAPTER EIGHT

I couldn't place Marissa's accent, so slight as to be almost undetectable. Her features and skin tone gave nothing away, either, only a vague foreignness. Andy, on our way to her office, had said he found her a bit of a cold fish. Corporate background. The board of trustees seemed convinced we needed a fundraiser rather than an educator for school principal. Now, sitting beside me at her glass-topped table, he gestured toward the eclectic art on the walls—silk-screen prints, tribal warrior masks, a charcoal sketch of the Eiffel Tower—and said to Marissa with something like sarcasm that she'd really made the place her own.

A work in progress, she said smoothly, her smile showing small, perfect teeth. With an equally perfect fingernail, glossed and tapering, she tapped the side of a festive-looking tin of dates. Please do help yourselves.

The dates were a gift from the family of a recent graduate, she said. The father had stopped in that morning—on a business trip from Dubai. She'd talked to him about the school's vision for a new wellness center, and he said it would give him great pleasure to support the plans with a significant donation. He *really* wants to do something for the school. He mentioned you in particular, Andy—apparently Song, who's back in Seoul now, doing an internship at her uncle's firm, thinks of you as the best science teacher she ever had.

Andy bit into a date. He'd observed, he said, again and again in his thirty-five years of teaching, that those students whose lives he could contribute very little to—because they were already so full— were the ones who seemed to think he'd given them a lot, whereas the 5 percent that he spent 95 percent of his time on, out of an obligation to make sure they learned *something*, rarely thanked him.

Oh, *Andy*. Marissa reached across and punched him lightly on the arm before turning to me. He's always so glum. Her eyes, generously outlined and shaded, gazed at me with commiseration. My stomach was a knot. On our walk over, Andy had been more talkative than usual, telling me his plans to ski over Thanksgiving break, how the snow had arrived just in time, how he'd probably in the next ten years require a knee replacement, and the forced joviality in his voice convinced me he was nervous on my behalf, that lying in wait for me in Marissa's office was the news that my job—and therefore my legal status in this country—would soon be coming to an end. Through the glass tabletop I watched her lift one slim leg and drape it elegantly over the other. In pearl earrings, fitted white trousers, and an iridescent blazer of crumpled silk—the kind I'd seen in the window displays of Cambridge boutique stores, which would cost me an entire paycheck to buy—she looked almost regal, a Western-educated royal from some little-known foreign kingdom, here to declaim my future.

Andy helped himself to another date. Marissa glanced at him, and when he continued to chew, she cleared her throat and addressed me herself. Technically, this is your midyear performance review. I'll cut to the chase and say we know these last months have been anything but easy—your first teaching job, your first job, really, postcollege; moving to a new city, in a country that's in many ways still unfamiliar to you—any of those things would be challenging on its own, and here you're facing them all at once. Do you agree, Andy?

Still chewing, Andy drummed his fingers on the table and gave me a sideways glance. In his old flannel shirt and khakis, his hair and beard obscuring his collar, he seemed not to care that he looked like a tramp—in fact, his reluctance to face Marissa suggested he found her immaculate look off-putting. He'd been pondering, he said, the discrepancies between what we as a school purported to value and what our actions declared. He remembered a faculty meeting early in his career where a consultant asked everyone to stand up and place themselves on a continuum across the length of the room, whose corners represented two extremes: Was their fundamental loyalty as teachers to their disciplines or to their students? At the time, he had, like most of his colleagues, chosen the latter and considered those who did the opposite to be in the wrong profession: Why choose to work with kids if they're not the reason you teach? Lately, though, watching their reactions to certain teachers—he indicated me with a wave of his hand—who didn't necessarily come from cultures that placed children on pedestals the way we did here, but who were diligent and hardworking, who had *standards* for what kids were supposed to know, he'd begun to feel that were he to do that whole exercise again, he might say that as a scientist his duty was at *least* as much to the discipline as to his students: watching me teach had made him aware of others' tendency to relax expectations in order to accommodate the kids, kids who seemed to be increasingly lost and fragile, with parents more protective and enabling. Were we—did we want to be—a coddling sort of school, where pleasing customers was more important than, well, molding an educated citizenry?

He seemed about to go on, but Marissa cut him off smoothly: It's not an either-or situation, Andy, as I'm sure you know. She swept out a notepad from under the slim stack of papers before her and addressed me again. It's about intangibles in your case. Not your qualifications, not your work ethic. With a shiny, heavy-looking pen she sketched, in four deft arcs, a pair of intersecting circles. This is you and this is our school. Obviously if we'd sensed no overlap at all between you and us, you wouldn't have been hired. But this intersection here—she shaded it in with brisk diagonal strokes—needs to be a bit larger before we can declare you a success. You might decide by the end of the year—or perhaps you've already decided—that you're not a creature of our habitat. Or we might decide that there's no way you can thrive here. At the moment, we're at a crossroads.

Andy coughed and said he wondered if there might be a more concrete way of approaching the problem.

Marissa shook her head majestically, her cloak of straight hair shifting between light and dark. The problem, she said, is an abstract one. Trying to make it concrete, to spell out a set of things you need to do, would not be helpful—those things wouldn't come naturally, you would strain to do them, or worse, you would do them and we'd still find you lacking. No, the solution lies with you and only you. You've been here long enough to know something of our rules—I don't mean school rules, I mean *rules*: of seeing, of listening, of thinking. Can you see and hear yourself through *our* eyes and ears? What about us through your—

Here Andy coughed again. Sorry, he said. With all due respect, if I were in her position, I would be feeling terrible right now because what you seem to be saying is that essentially she's not allowed to be herself.

Marissa spoke menacingly. Being oneself, everywhere one goes, Andy, is a luxury not everyone can afford.

Well then, he said, what, who, is she to be?

The version of her teaching self that goes here—she landed the nib of her pen once more in the overlap between the two circles. The folds of her silk blazer rippled and flashed; she bestowed on me again her flawless, glossy smile. As I was saying, what about you would seem to us—not objectionable, not wrong—but *quirky*? Now, can you turn that quirk into a strength? Can you expand your strengths so they obscure your weaknesses? Can you make yourself into an effective *brand*, in other words, and then sell it? Create a demand where none existed? Have students say, She's strict, she's tough, she's harsh—and we *love* her. She rapped her knuckles on the glass in emphasis, then extended her arms dramatically in my direction. *That's* the success story that someone like you can be in a place like this.

I sat transfixed. Andy leaned toward me with a look of concern, but I ignored him, focusing instead on Marissa, who met my gaze with narrowed eyes as if to be sure I'd understood what she'd said and also what she'd left unspoken.

■

At Whole Foods, on my way home from work, I chose a preassembled bouquet of carnations and a box of leaf-shaped chocolates wrapped in foil. When I surveyed the checkout counters, there was Zack—a shop assistant whose name I knew from the plastic badge pinned to his apron, who'd often smiled at me in a way I assumed meant nothing. He was the kind at college parties—athletic and clean shaven— whose expression as we talked would leave me thinking I'd been noticed and liked, until the second time we ran into each other, sometimes the very next day, when I'd be faced with a blank stare.

More Valentine's Day than Thanksgiving, Zack said, aiming his scanner at my flowers.

I would have liked to get the yellow tulips, I said, but I'd been invited to a Russian household, a colleague's, for Thanksgiving dinner, and Russians consider yellow flowers taboo save for funerals.

Will you go out with me sometime?

A part of me detached and stepped back to watch as another part reached for a pen, scribbled my number on the side of a receipt, and handed it to him.

■

Vinod, Olga's husband, and I were the only Indians in the bustle of Russians filling the house. He straddled a barstool at the kitchen counter, peeling a hard-boiled egg with great care, a barrel-chested man with slim, delicate hands and the profile of a toad: a flat, pock-marked nose, bulky shoulders that practically engulfed his neck, and absurdly skinny legs, his feet, in their fur-lined slippers, barely reaching the lower rung.

I came out of a lecture one day, he said—I was a PhD student in Moscow—and I saw this woman standing in a window with her back to me, cleaning the glass with a cloth. That was part of student life at the time, you know, sweeping, dusting, mopping. You can imagine what a shock it was for me, a middle-class Brahmin boy, having to do the tasks I'd been raised to think of as servants' work. The woman's hair was tied up in a scarf. I didn't see her face, just her silhouette against the glass, but it made me stop. It was the first and only time in my life I felt a physical blow from an invisible force. I tell you—he waved a shard of eggshell at me—if you're ever struck that way, don't resist it.

I recalled my encounter with the cashier boy the previous evening and wondered if what I'd felt was the thing Vinod was describing.

When she turned around, he continued, she didn't see me at first. I was in the shadow of a bookshelf, and her eyes had grown accustomed to the light outside. And then, I remember it so well, she blinked at me. I was all skin and bones back then, and she was standing on the windowsill, staring down at me. I must have looked like a twelve-year-old boy. She still blinks at me sometimes, like she can't believe what a slow coach she married. If I had her job, it would take me all day to correct one batch of homework. I used to assume she overlooked all kinds of errors, but one day I went through a batch of her geometry tests and couldn't find a single thing she'd missed.

I glanced at Olga, who was carrying a platter of green beans to the dining table. She seemed as relaxed and happy throwing a party as she did at work—her face flushed and smiling, her hair spilling from a high, untidy ponytail. I was reminded, hearing her rapid Russian, how she'd sounded the other day when I'd sat in on her geometry class. Her terse explanations were accompanied by energetic hand movements tracing ellipses and parabolas. Her students listened and watched attentively. They laughed at her jokes. Even if they didn't fully understand the postulates she was leading them through, I could tell they enjoyed being in her presence. Now, as she set the platter next to my carnations, which had settled unevenly in a glass vase, I told Vinod that what made Olga such a good teacher was not so much her efficiency but her charisma, her *brand*—how unique it was to her and therefore alluring to others. Marissa had made me realize that one's teaching self is a character one slips into—and the more the character is an extension of one's own personality, the more natural the performance.

Are you implying, he said, holding a peeled egg at eye level like a jeweler inspecting a Fabergé, that teaching is a form of acting?

You get up in front of an audience, I said, often a hostile one, and you try to hold their attention.

And you find this exercise difficult?

For me it was, I said, because the character I performed—a character not of my choosing but the result of my efforts to simply do my job—was one my audiences seemed reluctant to accept.

The flat nose twitched. He put the egg on a cutting board and ran it through with a knife. There are two paths ahead of you, he said: change your character or change your audience. America, he added, scooping out the grayish yolk, provides ample opportunity for both.

I sipped the sweet, malty kvass he'd poured for me and asked if he and Olga had come straight to America from Russia. In retrospect, he said, they should have done just that—it would have spared them a lot of difficulty, but after six straight years of living in the Soviet Union, he'd been homesick for India. Back then he'd anticipated that with his degree in electrical engineering he'd have no trouble getting a government job—he was still young enough to hold Nehru in high esteem. And of course, he wanted to introduce Olga to his country. They'd had a civil wedding in Moscow so she could obtain an exit visa, and he'd envisioned a gala celebration in India: temple ceremony, elephant, and all. He'd written to his parents informing them of his marriage, and when he received no reply assumed that either his letter or theirs had been lost in the mail. They'd be surprised, he anticipated, even shocked, by the news of his bride, but would be won over as soon as they met her. What happened was that he and Olga arrived in Hyderabad, took a taxi to the house he'd grown up in, and were turned away at the doorstep, Olga nearly fainting from the heat.

I had completely forgotten, Vinod said, as he fluffed the boiled yolks with a fork, living for so long in communist Russia, the choke hold that traditional religious thinking can have on a people. My father had traveled throughout Europe, spoke English and Russian fluently; my mother was a typist at a time when not that many Indian women had the opportunity to work. Yet, despite their education and exposure to the world, they told me they had no choice but to disown me because I'd refused to let them arrange my marriage, what my mother claimed was the greatest responsibility parents could ever have toward their child. We will not bless this marriage, she told us as we stood before her on the threshold with our luggage. Now, twenty years later, they're doting grandparents, they treat Olga like their daughter, they act as if it's always been like this, but I'll never forget how they spurned me that day. Standing before them, their own flesh and blood, being told I was a disgrace, that I was no longer their son, having them shut the door in my face—it was like I had just had the roots cut out from under me. I don't belong here anymore, I remember thinking, in fact I don't belong anywhere, which means—and this was what made the pain and anger I felt in the moment bearable—I am free to go anywhere I want and build a home.

He shouted Olga's name so loudly I jumped. She called back from the table, and after a brief exchange with him in Russian, rose to her feet and made her way toward us. From the refrigerator beside the counter, she took out a small glass jar and deposited it beside the cutting board where her husband was now meticulously dicing boiled egg whites with his knife. Draping an arm over his rounded shoulders, she looked at me and winked. I know, she said. Why can't he stand up and open fridge himself? Because I spoil him. Because husbands are like babies.

Vinod unscrewed the lid and showed me the glistening black caviar. It used to be plentiful, he said. In university they would pass around a jar several times the size of this one and eat the stuff by the spoonful. He gestured after Olga. The two of them had practically no money in India, he said, and no place to stay. Even if he hadn't lost touch with his childhood friends, they might have been wary about giving him and Olga shelter, coming as they did from families similar to his own—conservative and closed minded. His cousin, a salesman, rented an office near Charminar and let them use it as a hotel. They spent a week roaming the market by day and retiring to his cousin's sofa by night, until they ran into a former classmate from Moscow, a fellow Indian student who'd returned a year earlier and was working at an engineering firm. We didn't know each other well at university, Vinod said. But he took us in at once. Into his bachelor apartment, where we stayed for almost three months, until I was hired by ArkTech and we came here. He was furious at me for putting Olga in that position. A Russian woman! he kept saying. You bring a Russian woman to India, she's never experienced heat or crowds, and you expect her to live on the street!.

Vinod chuckled and shook his fist in mock fury. Before him, the eggs were now neat mounds of crumbled yolk and chopped white. He assembled for me, on a small piece of toast, a bit of each, along with minced red onion and a dab of caviar. When we arrived in America, he went on, there were fifty dollars in my pocket. We brought clothes and a samovar that Olga's mother had given us in Moscow. That's it. And look where we are now. He gestured at the kitchen and dining room, and, by extension, everything that lay beyond: the tended front lawn raked clean of fallen leaves, the cars in the driveway, the bedrooms overhead. Hard work and optimism, he said. There's no way you can go wrong if you have those things. I tell people all the time, you don't need government, you don't need welfare, if I could come to America with nothing and succeed, then why can't others? Olga tells me I shouldn't say such things at your school—that some people will find it offensive, that they will tell me I have *privilege*. Just because Olga and I make it look easy, as if we landed in America and that was that, instant success, instant wealth, doesn't mean we have *privilege*. His toad-like mouth flashed open and shut around a caviar-dressed square. We don't feel the need to dwell on our past hardships. We face them as part of life instead of complaining all the time the way some people do. As soon as you start thinking about others' advantages, you'll stop working hard, you'll lose motivation. He leaned closer to me and said, in a lowered voice, You seem unsure of yourself. Let me tell you, you can't afford to be unsure. Pick your path—he made a vertical blade of his hand and moved it back and forth in front of his face. Don't waver. With his other hand, he slapped the granite counter. The glass of caviar jumped and the column of toast squares looked ready to topple. That is how you conquer America.

CHAPTER NINE

At Out of Town News in Harvard Square, I flipped through a magazine and waited for Ram to join me. He'd called unexpectedly in the middle of the week. We marveled at the fact of us: two Bangalore kids who'd grown up on the same street, in neighboring houses shaded by the same mango tree, gone their separate ways, then converged within a mile of each other on the opposite side of the world. Neither of us could remember the last time we'd talked. We agreed we'd been more fixtures in each other's lives than friends, since when you're children, an age difference of three years is a chasm. And the coincidence of the two of us landing in Boston felt more extraordinary than it really was when you considered how people with similar backgrounds tended to move to similar places. The places accessible to them. America, he said, was becoming less accessible to people like us. He knew of a guy from his former school, a genius of sorts, who'd been granted admission and a full scholarship to Penn only to be denied a visa last June at the American consulate. In Ram's five trips through airport security this year, he'd been singled out to be searched every time. He was thinking of shaving off his beard. You have a beard? I said.

As he waved to me now from across Mass Ave., I saw the strip of dark stubble on his chin. His was the most complete transformation I'd ever seen: the scrawny, bashful, awkward boy from my childhood to the swarthy man striding toward me, arms outstretched. I found myself running to him, and when we collided by the curb, he embraced me, lifted me off the ground, and whirled me through the air. Can I tell you something? he asked once he'd set me back down and we were clutching at each other, breathless and giddy. I was thinking just now that if I'd happened to run into you on the street without knowing you were in Boston, I may not have recognized you. It's not that you've changed so much—you look the same, except for the haircut—it's that I've always associated you so much with Bangalore, there's no way you could exist for me outside of it. That's why it took me so long to get in touch. I just couldn't quite accept that you were here and not there. My mother says hello, by the way—she's been scolding me for not calling you. How are your parents?

We were standing close enough for me to smell the sharp tang of his aftershave. His face, like his body, had broadened and lengthened, his forehead and nose grown nicely prominent as if shaped by this new inner confidence. Large flecks of snow had started to drift and swirl about us. They clung to the woolen scarf knotted carelessly around his neck, and to his black, knee-length coat. His jeans were fashionably tight, his leather shoes polished, and I felt I understood completely why he'd hesitated to contact me. He'd metamorphosed into an attractive person, and I was someone who remembered a version of him he wanted nothing to do with.

I said I'd spoken to my parents the previous day, and they wanted to know whether I was applying to doctoral programs in physics, as they'd expected me to do before graduating and assumed was still my plan. The way they understood my decision to teach at a high school, I was merely taking a year off before returning to my studies.

So you're not? Ram asked.

I showed him the magazine I'd been leafing through. It was a literary journal, and I'd been reading a story by a writer who lived and taught in Boston, a Chinese man who wrote beautifully in English and whom I was planning to go see read at a bookstore the following week. If I decided to pursue a higher degree, I said, it would be in literature, or writing.

I expected him to smirk or roll his eyes. Instead he nodded. His girlfriend, he said, was a poet, in addition to being a medical intern. She wrote on the bus while commuting to work, she wrote between shifts, she wrote at home while waiting for the kettle to boil, and her poems were being published all over the place.

Where? I asked.

Online mostly, he said, as part of her friends' blogs. The hospital where she worked had recently included some of her verses in their employee newsletter. She had enough poems to fill several books now, and he'd been encouraging her to put together a collection. Forget about finding a publisher, I keep telling her. You can do it yourself. Design your own cover, find a printer, throw a launch party. I know nothing about poetry except the stuff we had to memorize in school—all that stupid Shakespeare and Wordsworth, millions of Indian children learning a poem about daffodils when there's not a single daffodil anywhere in India, but I do know—I minored in business studies after all—that throughout history successful entrepreneurs have started off small.

We were walking down Church Street toward Cafe Algiers on Brattle. The snow had put a layer of flannel over the paving stones by our feet. We didn't exactly live in a world, I said, where poems had commercial value.

But that's my point, he said and laughed. It was a peculiar sound, his laugh, still that high-pitched cry I remembered my mother once comparing to a jackal's. No wonder that boy has no friends, she liked to say, a laugh like that makes people think he's possessed by demons. We could easily live in that world, he said. It was completely arbitrary what things had value and what didn't. If there was a lesson America had taught the world, it was that you can make a burger from nothing but crap and convince millions, billions of people to line up for it. Yoga was another example. The other day, after ignoring the studio down the street from his house for more than two years, he'd walked in on a whim and taken a class. The entire time, he was in disbelief. He'd paid fifteen dollars—close to seven hundred rupees—to have a white woman take him through poses he knew just from having grown up where he had—whose names she couldn't even say properly. The exercises had been around for millennia, could be looked up in any number of books. But people paid happily to be led through a few of them and hear a bunch of new-age garbage about mind-body connection and prana and whatnot, in a stuffy room smelling of patchouli. He enjoyed the class, he was embarrassed to say. His body felt good afterward. He'd be going back for more. He was getting fed white people's versions of his own forefathers' wisdom and knowledge, and he was lapping it up. It was absurd, but living in the West meant living in an ether of absurdity. He'd traveled to England the previous year, his first trip to the land of our colonizers. In the British Museum, looking up at a statue of a dancing Shiva, he was aware that he was standing over several underground floors filled with similar loot, some artifacts too valuable to even be put on display and all from his—from our—country. Scattered throughout this small island were vast hoardings of pillage worth more than entire nations, some in vaults, others part of public displays as blatant as the prosperity he saw everywhere around him, the efficiencies and appurtenances of Western living, all made possible by the looting and impoverishment of his motherland among others, and were he to ask a museum guide directions to galleries containing more loot, the answer would be delivered cheerfully, warmly even, in a plummy British accent. Were he to say, This is loot—shouldn't you give it back? the guide would look at him as if he'd suggested something preposterous, and were he to attempt to take an Indian artifact back to India and say to the police, when they arrested him for theft—or to a judge, assuming he was even granted a hearing—that all he was doing was returning loot to the place it was looted from, the same part of the world, incidentally, where the word "loot" had its origins, at best he'd be treated like a harmless loony. So, Ram concluded, I've decided to just enjoy life here in the West, to dive into anything and everything that gives me pleasure, and not to think too much about origins and histories, because if I do, I'll go mad.

At the entrance to our restaurant, we were handed menus. I led the way upstairs, to the corner table by a hookah, where I'd eaten a falafel roll by myself the week before. Ram looked around in approval. He'd been wanting to spend more time in this part of Cambridge, he said. The MIT area had its own gravitational field, hard to escape sometimes.

A waitress with the physique and scraped-back hair of a ballerina approached us. We ordered plates to share, and coffees. I'll have a Turkish, he said, shedding his coat and scarf to reveal a waffle-knit shirt contoured by the muscles of his chest and shoulders. No real news from home, he said, except Hippy died in October.

How old was he? I asked.

Twelve.

Is that old for a dog?

Oh, I wish he'd died years earlier. He stared for some moments at the table, and in my mind's eye I saw Hippy pulling him along, Ram tilting backward as if he were on water skis, his then-skeletal frame fighting to stay upright as the dog, a tall, wiry animal, whipped and bucked. I must have been eleven at the time, and as I walked past the dog and Ram, who would have been fourteen, I sensed, from the torture on his face—teeth bared, chin tucked, eyes screwed shut—that his desperation was deeper than a mere physical struggle.

He hadn't talked about Hippy to anyone, Ram said, not even his girlfriend. There was no way to tell the story without making himself and his family seem pathetic, twisted even—but since I'd known them since childhood, I'd understand what he was about to tell me.

I couldn't say I knew his family all that well, I said, especially his father. Hippy had always seemed rather ferocious.

Ram leaned toward me. Above us on the wall, a patchwork of mirrors reflected the scene outside. White sky and falling snow formed a picture brighter but less distinct than the view through the window. As a pup, he said, Hippy had, with his mournful eyes and little whimpers, triggered in him an overwhelming urge to cuddle and squeeze. Being an only child with no extended family nearby and few friends, he was primed to smother any creature bound to him. Had Hippy's temperament been different, maybe the dog could have helped him learn the balances of love, its boundaries and flexibilities. But it should have been obvious the day Hippy arrived—a rat-sized, grubby thing brought in by the maidservant, who'd found him in a ditch outside her house—that he was an aggressive, independent creature, not prone to bonding with humans. Ram's parents had grown exasperated with his demands for a pet. Are you sure you want this dog? they asked as he took the puppy from the maidservant and let it gnaw his finger with its tiny teeth, sharp enough to draw blood. If so, he's your responsibility. Don't expect us to do anything. You asked for a pet, you look after it, otherwise he'll have to go. Understand?

It's a common story, he went on, for a dog, brought into a home at the urging of a child, to wheedle its way into the parents' affections. The version of the tale that took place in his family was rather perverse. He'd always felt his parents' disapproval of him more than he had their love. He wanted something warm, furry, and playful that would lick and nestle up to him and make him feel he mattered. The dog's tendency to snap and snarl unnerved him. Why? he would find himself saying. Why do you bite me when I love you? Then it became: No matter how much you bite me, I will love you. He would clamp his hand around Hippy's muzzle and snuggle him harder, which of course became more difficult as the animal grew. He wished he'd been able to say to his parents, We're just not a good match, Hippy and I, all we do is cause each other frustration, let's take him to the shelter and be done with it. That he couldn't acknowledge such a thing showed the magnitude of his desperation to know he was capable of loving and being loved in return. He was trapped—in the same way Hippy was trapped. It was impossible to let the dog roam free in the yard like a normal pet because he'd attack anyone who came through the gate—and since his mother refused to have him in the house, he had to be chained to the porch. Literally chained. The day Ram and his father went to the pet shop to buy the heaviest-gauge shackles, the owner asked if they had an Alsatian. Mongrel,

Ram said, and the man insisted it must be a Rajapalayam, bred to hunt wild boar.

His father, Ram continued, decided that if Hippy was by nature rebellious, then they must accept him as so. After his initial insistence that Hippy had to be Ram's pet—that if Ram wanted to keep him, he would have to feed him, walk him, clean up after him, and if he failed to do these things, confirming that he was, as his parents had always complained, irresponsible and lazy, then the pup would have to go—his father developed a sort of obsession with Hippy. He started to come home early from work—he had never come home early to spend time with Ram or Ram's mother—and he and the dog would bully each other. Rile each other up. Deliberately. Hippy hated having his nose touched, so Ram's father would slap him about the face, then yank his hands away before Hippy could bite off his fingers. Or they'd fight. Hippy would get up on his hind legs and lunge. Man and beast would lock arms and dance around the yard. It was a strange sight, the two of them, going at each other like wrestlers, full of concentration, teeth bared, snarling. Watching them, Ram couldn't help feeling that Hippy was a stand-in for him. His dad had often tried to get him to do the things that he as a boy had been subjected to in Army School: wake up at five in the morning, run three kilometers, bathe in cold water. The fact, Ram said, that I would stay up late listening to music on my Walkman made him mad. The fact that I'd get teased mercilessly at school—he said it was entirely my problem, that I'd better find a way of standing up for myself if I wanted to get anywhere in the world. I never really answered back when he said those things. I would start to cry, and nothing disgusted him more than tears. Perhaps what he was really fighting was his own father, who beat him regularly and ultimately drank himself to death.

I remembered Hippy's wailing, I said. I hadn't known a dog was capable of making such a sound.

We had him neutered, Ram said, but it made absolutely no difference. He kept biting and scratching and having these wailing fits at all odd hours. My father found them funny. He's singing, he would say. He's a musical dog. The neighbors in the apartment complex behind us complained to my mother one day. If you can't stop the noise, we'll call the municipal corporation and have them take him away. My mother threw her own grand fit. You should have seen her that evening, stamping her feet and shaking her fists at us, screaming. Do you know what my life is like? Having the neighbors blame me for the racket your dog is making? This animal I never wanted in the first place? My father shrugged and said, Okay, he'll come with me to work from now on and I'll have the office boy take care of him. My mother continued to rage. It was like a valve had blown. The two of you don't give a damn about me, you've never shown any appreciation for me, ever. You eat your breakfast and you take off in the morning, you leave me to cook for you, clean up after you, wash your clothes. I'm thinking of running away. My father made this flicking motion with his hand as if he were batting a fly and said, You're the one who's wailing now. I expected him to turn to me and say, This is all your fault, see? You're the one who wanted a dog, all this drama is happening because of you, you're responsible for destroying this family.

The waitress returned with our food, coffee, and a pitcher of water. As she maneuvered into our corner, the tray, held between her palm and shoulder, began to tilt. There was a brief rustle of silverware, but the next moment everything righted as she bent from the knees and set her burden on the neighboring table. Hot sauce, please, Ram said when she asked if there was anything else she could bring. Am I airing too much dirty laundry? he asked me. Have I put you off?

The waitress distracted me, I said. I was thinking how much static friction the tray would need to exert on the dishes to keep them from sliding. This is what teaching has done to me: put my subconscious on alert at all times for examples to bring to the classroom. A colleague of mine who teaches English told me the other day that it wasn't possible anymore for her to read a book for pleasure: the instinct to formulate questions for her students refused to be silenced.

We started on our soup, Ram frowning as he ate quickly, scraping the bottom of the bowl each time he plunged his spoon into the lentils. When he finished, he wiped his mouth slowly with a napkin. I've put you off, he said. I apologize. I felt like I had to tell someone. It's partly why I called you last week. My mother sent me your number months ago. At the time I was irritated—my first response to anything my mother does. She told me your mum was worried about you being so far away and living by yourself. I thought, So what? It's not like Pavitra and I were ever close growing up. If her mum is worried about her, why is that my problem? Then Hippy died. It affected me more than I would have expected.

Hearing about Hippy, I said, reminded me of a time when I, too, desperately wanted a pet. I was in middle school and a voracious reader of Enid Blyton and James Herriot, and every time I asked for a dog my mother told me that just as I harbored delusions about steak-and-kidney pudding being delicious, I'd also been led to believe that owning a dog was all fun and games. She was terrified of most animals, so this was the main reason we could never have one. But she also believed there was something ludicrous about people wanting animals for company. When we visited friends' houses where there were dogs or cats, she stiffened, which never failed to attract the animals' curiosity. They'd make a beeline for her and set her yelping with fear. On our way home she would wonder aloud at how people spent money and time raising these four-legged creatures who barked and whined and licked and left their smells and hair on everything. It was the licking that really got to her—the fact that human beings, grown-ups, would allow themselves to be basted in a dog's saliva. We rented the movie *Beethoven* once, on videocassette, and the sight of the Saint Bernard slobbering on everyone drove her from the room.

Ram chuckled. He went after his chicken shawarma, his sunny confidence intact again, and I wondered if the secret to his transformation from a sullen, sulky boy was that he'd learned to skip over worries and disappointments before they fully sank in. No doubt, I said, he knew about the Kailash Saint Bernards?

The what?

I'd been walking through the cantonment area once—probably on my way to some interschool quiz competition—when I found myself in front of the Kailash mansion, and facing what looked to be a bear, an enormous animal with a rippling coat of thick fur. But there was something odd about the way it was sitting. Bears sat squarely on their behinds, feet splayed—from what I remembered of Winnie-the-Pooh. Then the thing barked, and I realized it was a dog. My god, I thought, a Saint Bernard, in Bangalore. Then a second Saint Bernard came running up alongside. And then another and another until there were eight of them lined up behind the rails, jowls shaking, barking in synchrony, ropes of drool stretching from their mouths, a reverberating, mournful chorus. I learned that Kailash housed the dogs in separate air-conditioned kennels and flew them every year to Switzerland on his private planes. This was about seven years ago now, when the Kailash mansion was the largest in the city. As Ram probably knew, it was being dismantled. Kailash's son was going to have it reconstructed, stone by stone, on the fiftieth floor of the skyscraper he was building, part of a complex of high-rises near Cunningham Circle. A private elevator would take him and his Mercedes to the top, where the next generation of Saint Bernards would have penthouse kennels.

Ram put down his fork and chewed thoughtfully. The last time he'd been in Bangalore, foundations for the high-rise complex I'd mentioned were just starting to be dug—he recalled the road closures and dust. He had no idea the mansion was to be taken apart and reassembled—not that it surprised him, given what he knew of the Kailash scion and his wealth—but then, he was hardly up to date on what was going on in Bangalore, or India for that matter, because he got most of his news from the media here. He had no intention of ever returning home. The day his parents had that fight over Hippy was the day Ram began to see he had no choice but to leave, that if he didn't, he'd turn into his father. So he doubled down on his studies. He'd wanted to get into Pilani, or St. Stephen's in Delhi. Both long shots. At some point he learned that the acceptance rate for international students at American colleges was much higher, so he studied for the SATs. They gave me a ridiculous amount of money, Brandeis did, he said with his hyena laugh. I guess being from India makes it easy to qualify for aid.

It surprised me, I said, that there wasn't more resentment among American students, so many of whom had to take out large loans to attend college, that people like us, middle-class Indians with universities of our own to go to, would be welcomed so lavishly here, in a country that wasn't ours.

Ram seized his fork and speared a hunk of meat. With his elbows thrust outward, he seemed determined to take up as much space as he could on the narrow bench. America needed people like us, he said. We were what allowed those who were here before us to lead the complacent, sheltered lives they'd grown used to. It was a simple principle for a rich country: entice capable, qualified, industrious people from around the world to come, and then let them do their thing so that the locals, the folks who've been here for generations and no longer have to prove themselves, can take it easy. Don't waste any energy, he told me, worrying about whether you are worthy of being here. The question should be whether America is worthy of *you*.

All I knew at the moment, I said, was that I had to work hard to keep my job. The school's petition for my H-1B visa had been approved, I'd learned the previous day, but if by the end of the year my superiors concluded I wasn't a good fit for the institution, my contract would not be renewed. If that happened, I'd be forced to leave.

So, home is here now?

I wasn't prepared to say that.

But you don't want to go back?

Not yet.

He grasped the long handle of the ibrik. I'd never ordered Turkish coffee before; I watched him pour the dark, syrupy liquid into his cup with an ease that suggested he'd made a habit of it. Perhaps why you and I are really here, he said, is to be left alone. We can try new things in an empty arena, with no one around to pounce on us with their interrogations and mockery. We can hear ourselves think for the first time. For you it's a matter of your writing career—you've always struck me as ambitious, wanting to be at the top in whatever you do. At home you'd have been reluctant to try something your family was suspicious of, but you can do that here. For me it's more a matter of lifestyle. I've never been driven to work hard just for the sake of working hard. I work because I have to. What I live for is to be a connoisseur of different experiences. I'm already getting tired of Boston. In a year or two I hope to move to San Francisco or Boulder. Biotech gives me flexibility to find a job in any city I care to live in and earn enough to explore what the region has to offer. I've spent a total of seven years now in the Northeast. I've learned how to ski and ice-skate, I've traveled by ferry to at least twenty islands off the coast of Maine, I've hiked all the major mountains of New Hampshire and Vermont, and I've dined at eight of the ten best restaurants in Boston as rated by Zagat.

He and his girlfriend, he went on, were avid dancers; they rarely let more than a week go by without a visit to a nightclub. He had dreams of learning how to surf in Hawaii, of spending days wine-hopping in Napa. His motto was to never settle anywhere. At some point he hoped to become a consultant. Then he would be able to plan his life around where he wanted to be at each time of year. Reykjavik in midsummer, New Orleans for Mardi Gras, Madagascar for Christmas. As he gulped the last of his coffee, there was something in the way he did it—the jerk of his chin, the clatter of the empty cup as he set it back on the saucer—that brought back my image of him as a boy entwined with the dog's leash, Hippy dragging him along the street. Now he spread his arms along the top of the bench, crossed one ankle over the other knee, and leaned back as if he were basking. I am free, he seemed to be telling himself. I am free, I am free, I am free.

Would his girlfriend be willing to move around with him? I asked. Did she have a similar wanderlust?

She was attached to New England, he said. Her parents and siblings lived in the area and she was, unlike him, family oriented. He suspected he might never have a life partner, that like the places he visited, relationships were things he'd always be passing through.

And what about you? he asked. Have you had time to do any dating?

The only thing that qualified as a date, I told him, was a dinner I'd had weeks earlier with a cashier boy who'd asked me out while scanning my groceries. He was a cellist by training. Over seafood paella in the South End he told me that he'd developed an aversion to his instrument once he realized he could never truly own any of the pieces he'd learned to play. You master something and it's still not yours, he said. It belongs to this dead white guy, ultimately, and here I am, a living white guy playing a dead white guy's music. He kept talking about conquest as this basic human need. His eyes seemed unable to focus on one point, a tic that matched the constant tapping of his foot on the floor, which set our table vibrating. He told me he was on a mission to taste every type of legume in the world; he was currently bidding online for a bag of heirloom lima beans so rare there were less than five pounds of it harvested each year, in one tiny region of Italy.

Beans? He's bidding on *beans*? As Ram slapped his thigh and let loose his preternatural laugh, I recalled how Zack had helped himself one by one to all three of the shrimp that had come arranged in a trefoil pattern in the center of our paella, legs and feelers intact. Maybe "conquest" is the wrong word, he said as he lifted the third shrimp to his mouth with his fingers. Through the translucent carapace I watched his tongue and teeth do their work. He made sure to excavate every morsel of meat, stretching the joints to get at the bits along the spine. "Own" might be a better way of putting it, he concluded, dropping the mangled remains onto a small plate, alongside the clamshells he had already dug clean.

The best part of the evening, I said to Ram, was the two of us taking the T back to Cambridge. I liked being seen with my white companion in public, liked especially when Indian people saw us. A stern auntie in her silk sari, guys speaking in Tamil on the train—I wanted them to see me tossing away our culture by crossing into another. It was like that moment in the Flannery O'Connor story, when the man on the bus fantasizes about the day he'd bring home a Black woman for no other reason than to shock his racist mother. In the end, I said, it was all as petty as it sounded, especially considering that my family would be more open to my dating a white man than an Indian of low caste, or a Muslim.

Ram looked me up and down with something like approval. He'd never known, he said, that I had this rebellious streak. He'd always thought, seeing me in my school uniform, with my thick glasses and neat ponytails, that I was the quintessential good Indian girl: studious, well behaved, conforming. If you hadn't left, he said, you'd be an engineer now, earning a decent salary at some boring company, and your parents would be starting to fret about finding a good match. The only thing more absurd than staying here would be for you to go back.

I let him pay the bill, and we descended the stairs and stepped outside, into a soft layer of snow already turning to gray slush. The flakes had stopped falling, the cleansed air prickled my skin, and the edges and corners of everything around us seemed clearer and sharper against the white sky as we embraced lightly, almost hurriedly, promising to keep in touch from now on.

CHAPTER TEN

In the large central room of Elena's apartment, I helped her collapse the futon into a bed. You're welcome to the desk, too, she said brusquely. Jen never uses it. When we first moved in, we were all excited about having a work area separate from our bedrooms, but it turns out she prefers the kitchen table and the only place I can study is in bed. Something about having my legs stretched out under the covers. It's how I did homework as a teenager, how I typed my thesis in college—why did I think in law school my habits would suddenly change?

From a wall closet she pulled down a comforter and a set of linens in plastic casings that crackled and squeaked as she unzipped them. I was tempted to help as she unfurled a sheet, but her nimble movements made it clear I'd only be a hindrance. My hands were still stiff with cold from the walk over. I thanked her again for letting me stay at such short notice. I couldn't believe, I added, that it was only my second time in her apartment, that the last time we'd gotten together was at the end of August.

She shook the comforter out of its noisy bag. You buy renters' insurance, I assume? For your stuff?

The only stuff worth anything was my computer, I said, and I'd had it with me the whole time. I was aware my voice sounded faint and toneless. All day I'd felt as if I were trapped behind glass, watching my life proceed at a distance. It was the end of fall term. That morning

I'd lain in bed watching the gray sky through the slats of the window blinds and thinking about how, starting tomorrow and for the next two weeks, I could sleep in, read, write, and fill the time doing whatever I wanted, but the more I tried to imagine being on vacation, the more impossible it felt. As I was eating lunch at my office desk and grading lab reports, an early dismissal was called on account of the blizzard, originally forecast to strike at night, now advancing more quickly than expected. In the ensuing scramble I asked a colleague to drop me off at Porter Square, and from there I walked to Café Rustica through the first drifting flakes, sat at a table, and opened my computer. My fingers tapped the keys without stopping. I couldn't remember the last time full sentences had marched out of me with volition of their own, and when I finally looked away from the screen, I had to remind myself where I was. By then the sky was dark and the snowfall had thickened. I trudged in a happy daze through the shin-high drifts of powder, across this new landscape where the old borders of streets and curbs had been erased, a daze that must have blunted the icy wind—and the shock, when I arrived at the landlord's mother's house, of seeing the main branch of the maple lying across the smashed roof and dormers, illuminated by the lights of a fire engine on the scene.

I repeated my thanks to Elena for letting me be her roommate again.

What did you expect? That I'd say, Sorry, can't take you, good luck finding somewhere to sleep, it's not my problem if you freeze to death?

I didn't know how long it would be, I added, before I could move back to my place.

She gazed at me solemnly. I have to say, she said, hearing you describe the heating problems and the missing tiles in the bathroom and all that, I couldn't help but think, This is why she never invites me over—she's embarrassed. And I was a bit irritated by that, to tell you the truth. I kept thinking, Aren't we friends? Did those four years in college together mean nothing? Is she really afraid I'd think less of her because of her living circumstances? I talked with Jen about it, and we agreed you're just someone who likes to appear in control at all times, who won't ask for help unless you're literally—I don't know—on the street?

The reason I'd never invited her to mine, I said, had everything to do with the landlord's mother and sister. I didn't know how much of the old woman's treatment of me was attributable to her advanced age, but I could never shake the sense that she both resented my presence and found me intriguing. I suspected, after finding things moved around in my room, that she'd climbed upstairs at least once and rifled through my belongings. And then there was her daughter, Val, who every time she visited the house acted like my existence was a threat to her mother. My fear of angering the two of them had dissuaded me from ever inviting someone over: if they considered me a trespasser, how would they react to a guest? I'd found them outside the house that evening, in the dark, Val helping her mother into the car. It took me several moments to discern, through the blowing snow, the fallen branch behind them. Val saw me and slammed the passenger door. She was bareheaded, and the snow had clumped her hair into white tentacles. She shook her fist. My mother could have been killed in there, she screamed. You don't give a damn about her or the house—if you did, you'd have gotten home early, or at least called to make sure she was okay. My brother doesn't give a damn either. I've been telling him for how many years now to take a chain saw to that branch? No tree should ever be allowed to grow so close—but he doesn't listen to what I have to say. He's not even here, he's on the Cape gallivanting with friends. I'm the one who has to deal with this mess.

Charming, Elena said. I'd have given her an earful right there. I'd have said, Lady, the thing that's a mess is you, you need to adjust your medications. I was worried about you living there from the very beginning, as soon as I heard you hadn't signed a proper lease and that the place was run-down. Sure, I was envious of your rent, but I thought, I'd rather pay more if it means a reliable living situation. She leaned sideways against the doorframe, willowy and elegant in her oversize sweatshirt and black tights, and I was aware suddenly of my own bedraggled clothes and wet hair.

That branch, I said, reminded me of the spate of falling trees in my home city, roots giving way amid the widening of roads and the laying of fiber-optic cables and crushing people to death, at least a dozen in the past month, my mother had claimed when we'd talked last. How ignominious would it have been for a Bangalorean to travel all the way to Boston and get killed by a stupid tree?

Elena grimaced in a way that made it clear she didn't appreciate my humor. I'd called her from a convenience store on Hampshire Street, my phone having died in the cold. Sure, she'd said at once. Come over, stay as long as you need. She'd been the same way in college: easy generosity that lured me to let my guard down, to confide things that she then would react to in deflating ways. I'm going to make some dinner, she said now.

My phone buzzed from the living room floor, where earlier I'd plugged it into an outlet. The landlord's name lit up on the screen. He said he was marooned on the Cape until the storm passed, which wouldn't be until early morning. If I needed a place to stay, I was welcome to go to his Somerville house and let myself in with the key I'd find under the doormat—that was all he could offer at the moment. His clipped tone reminded me of our phone conversation months earlier, when he'd said he understood my situation but could not, unfortunately, help. I was staying with a friend in Cambridgeport, I told him, and he replied, Good, then I'll call you once I've had a chance to look at things tomorrow.

In the kitchen I found Elena with her back to me, filling a pot with water. Gusts were rattling the windowpane by the stove. The ceiling lights flickered. There are some candles in there, she said, gesturing with her elbow to a drawer. And a flashlight. Can you get them out?

Anything else I can do? I asked, but she set the pot on the stove as if she hadn't heard me, then walked across the room into the pantry. I looked over to see if there were any dirty dishes I could wash, but the sink was empty. When she reemerged with a box of spaghetti and a jar of sauce, I asked what her opinion was, given that I didn't have renters' insurance: Should I ask the landlord to compensate me for any damage? To refund me the month's rent, or at least part of it? He seemed a reasonable, well-meaning sort. He'd taken an interest in me as a writer, treated me to tea once. There'd been a time, early on, when I'd wondered about his motives, but I no longer had reason to.

She put the items on the counter and spoke over her shoulder. Isn't it obvious what he's up to? He gave you no lease to sign—you realize that's totally illegal, right? He knows it, believe me. And he knows damn well the place had maintenance issues. He wouldn't be able to register the property as a rental unit without getting those seen to, but he didn't want to deal with them, so he chose to rent to you under the table. And went to lengths to convince you of his kindness and generosity so that in a time like this, you'd let him off the hook. If I were you, I'd threaten to sue.

Such an American response, I said, suing.

Well, you're in America, she said, opening the jar lid with a pop, and I was reminded of the time in college when she'd said, after reading a story of mine, that it wasn't clear why my character, a young girl, would be so shy and polite. I'd protested that I couldn't imagine her any other way because in the society I'd grown up in, which was the same society as that of my character, it would be unthinkable for a child to be rude to her elders, even when they were nasty to her. But *I'm* not of that society, Elena said patiently. The kid in your story is so timid and has such a formal way of speaking that she'll stand out over here as a candidate for therapy. That's your American perspective, I shot back. Sure, it's my perspective, she'd said. I imagine if I wrote a story and showed it to someone from India, they'd think my characters were nuts. You're *here* now, aren't you? If you were *there* and writing for folks *there*, that would be one thing. If you come *here*, then you can't expect people to understand everything you're saying about the place you're from. It's like when I traveled to Morocco with my mother. We were careful to cover our heads and not wear short skirts and things like that. There are obnoxious Americans who flout those customs, but when you're a guest somewhere, the expectation is that you'll adapt to the local culture, not the other way around.

Watching her shake the brittle noodles into the boiling water, I again felt the gulf between us, hidden, that I could pretend didn't exist until I tripped over the edge.

Can I just say one thing? she said. I hope you won't take offense. But I need to say this: I'm a bit sad we had to wait for this emergency to get together. I feel like I've been the one constantly reaching out to you, leaving you voice messages, trying again, and when you do respond, it's always to say you can't meet up. I keep telling myself, It's not that she doesn't *want* to see me, it's that she's busy. But then I remember how you spent your breaks on campus, by yourself basically, just you in our room. There's no way I could ever do that. Maybe at some level you don't need friends the way I do.

That's not true, I said. I really have been busy.

The lights flickered again as she drained the contents of the pot into a colander. We sat at the table and shook Parmesan cheese over our steaming plates of spaghetti and microwaved sauce, watching the granules melt and dissolve. I wanted to tell her what I wished I'd said when we were in college, that people in India grow up reading books by English, European, and American writers, writers who'd never considered it their job to help little brown children in the tropics understand cold, white, Western worlds, yet we read them without complaining, with joy even. When we didn't understand something, we looked it up. Or just accepted it as something foreign and carried on reading. I tasted the food, which was bland but warming, as the wind continued to howl and snowflakes chattered at the window. Thank you, I said again. Thank you for letting me stay.

Stay as long as you like, she said with a shrug. You're my guest.

■

The tree, said the landlord when he called the next morning, was declared perfectly healthy by an arborist not that long ago. I used to swing from it as a boy. My father hung a tire for me—one of the last things he did before he left—and I'd swing all the way across what's now the side porch. So you can imagine what I felt seeing that branch snapped like a breadstick. Never in a million years would I have thought it could go through the roof like that. I'm looking at the house right now, my childhood home, you know, and never in a million years could I have predicted it would be wrecked in a snowstorm. He'd been thinking lately, he went on, how warm the winter had been, how when he was growing up there always used to be snow on the ground by his birthday, but now we could get to mid-December with scarcely a dusting. Let's please have a nor'easter, he'd thought several times in the past weeks and then last night, looking out of the window in Falmouth, he saw what could only be described as torrential snow and it reminded him of being in Goa when the monsoon broke, the most dramatic weather he'd ever witnessed— low, dark clouds advancing from the sea, getting larger and darker, the first drops turning to steam before they hit the ground, and then just like that, summer was over, extinguished by a rumbling deluge. Winter in Boston used to be a gradual thing, he said, every day a little cooler, a bit of frost here and there followed by a hard freeze, not balmy Decembers and then monsoon snows.

Holding the phone between my ear and shoulder, I filled a bowl from the opened box of fortified cornflakes I'd found in Elena's pantry. The sun was out, and through the kitchen window I could see clumps of snow dropping from trees into an ocean of white. A few people had come out to shovel, wading thigh deep across the submerged sidewalk and street. My head felt foggy. I'd slept badly, having woken several times during the night to scribble down the speech I imagined giving to the landlord—how it wasn't his fault the tree had fallen, but he needed to acknowledge that the accident had severely disrupted my life as his tenant. While I didn't have the American impulse to sue, I did believe it was his obligation to make up for it. I wanted to sound calm and firm, but felt increasingly nervous as he spoke. I'm just heading back to the car, he said. He'd set out at five o'clock, as the storm was waning and still the drive to his mother's house took well over three hours. But I did manage to get in, he said, and go upstairs. You'll be happy to know that your room—my old room—is pretty intact. Doesn't look like there's any damage inside. The attic caved in, but the ceiling held.

So my things were okay?

As far as he could tell, they were.

It didn't seem, I said, that I'd be able to move back in.

True. Not until repairs are done, and I'm not sure how long those will take. Sounds like you have a place to stay at the moment.

I wasn't interested in moving back to his mother's, I said, even after repairs were finished. I asked him to refund me this month's rent.

Of course, he said. Goes without saying.

I poured milk from the refrigerator over the cornflakes and placed the bowl in the microwave to warm a bit. It was my first time renting a place in America, I told him, and in retrospect, I never should have agreed to move into his mother's house without a proper lease.

I listened to his breathing, heavy with exertion, and what sounded like the crunch of snow underfoot. I have a suggestion, he said. You remember the room I showed you in the spring? The current occupant is moving out before New Year's and looking for a subletter. I can let you have it for 950 a month.

The microwave beeped. Six hundred, I said, surprised at how quickly the words came to me. It's what I'd been paying and would have kept paying had that tree—his tree—not fallen.

I waited for him to say my demands were unreasonable. Instead he grunted and answered in his clipped way, six hundred a month for the remainder of the lease.

My heart rose despite the congealed mess in my bowl—I'd allowed the milk to boil. In my mind's eye I saw the Fayette Street building, its wood-paneled foyer, the stairs that creaked, the airy apartment, and the elegant, light-filled bay window. That's where I would write.

PART III

CHAPTER ELEVEN

I took the Red Line to Park Street and spotted my cousin as soon as I stepped out of the station. She was standing by one of those souvenir stalls at the edge of the Common, her profile to me, bareheaded, hands pushed deep for warmth into the pockets of a thin coat. The day was bright but frigid: snow from last week's storm was still heaped everywhere, sidewalks patched with dirty ice. She seemed to be observing with some longing the stall's woolen hats and gloves, most of them Red Sox memorabilia, and I felt protective of her—my little cousin who had never before traveled off the subcontinent, so had no conception of what it meant to be cold, whose brand-new clothes, all purchased no doubt for the occasion of her trip to Boston, offered little insulation from the late-December chill. Her shoes were shiny patent leather and her jeans were baggy, the kind I used to wear as a teenager in Bangalore. Her voice was nearly a shriek as she greeted me, and I wondered for a moment if women's voices in India were higher than they were here. She said she felt fine, no jet lag at all, she'd slept in the Dubai airport lounge and again on the flight to Logan, and then slept until five thirty that morning, at her uncle's in Quincy. He sends his regards, she said. He remembers you as a baby, when he visited your parents' house.

Her grin showed protruding teeth with gaps. As we walked down Tremont to the gathering point for guided tours of the Freedom Trail,

I apologized for not being able to give her a place to stay. When I was still living at the landlord's mother's, she'd asked if she could crash with me, at least until she found accommodations of her own, and I'd said, regretfully, that my place was too small. The house had spare rooms, but I'd shied from the prospect of a family member staying there, the old lady watching us with her hostile, curious gaze, my cousin's singsong speech and her accent, much more pronounced than mine—it was the heavy Tamilian accent that even in Bangalore would have been mimicked and mocked—the landlord's sister scolding me in front of my cousin, implicating us both in the neglect of her mother, and then my cousin reporting to her parents, who'd relay to mine, that I was living in a shabby room in a shabby American house whose owners were scary and rude, prompting my mother to call and chastise me, saying she didn't understand why I was living like a vagabond in America—was this my long-term plan?

Since we had half an hour before the next tour, I led her to a Starbucks on a side street. Hot chocolate, she said eagerly, and I ordered two. She uncapped her drink and licked the whipped cream off the lid. Too good, she said, beaming, the first time she was having a proper hot chocolate, it was one of the things she wanted to make sure she tried here before going back to India—the other was pizza. She wrapped her hands around the paper cup. We were sitting on barstools by the window, her thick braid, bereft of the string of jasmine she would pin to it at home, hanging unadorned to her waist. There were gloves and a hat in her bag, she said; she'd just wanted to fully feel the cold, the coldest cold she'd ever felt in her life. Crazy, she said as she clutched her cup, still shivering but smiling, lips drawn back over her misaligned teeth, her large, lustrous eyes roving with excitement. A family friend in Chennai who'd spent many years in Canada had told her to practice for the winter by sitting in the fridge, but she suspected no refrigerator would have prepared her for cold like this. She'd never felt her hands and the tips of her ears burn with cold, hadn't known it was possible. It's crazy, she repeated. But she wanted the experience, it was part of the whole adventure of coming here. Her internship didn't begin until after New Year's, and she planned to spend the next few days just exploring and taking in the sights, because once the work started, as she'd been told by former interns—those students from her college in Chennai who'd been through the same eight-month program—she'd be spending all her time on campus, in the genetics laboratory run by the Indian professor who'd funded the bulk of her stay. It wasn't that he himself was particularly demanding—on the contrary, he had a reputation for being laid back and jovial; it was that she had to make sure she obtained some real results that she could report on when she went home in August, since, unlike her peers who would've done projects at local labs and institutions, she would be under extra scrutiny for having gone abroad. *You went to America and all, and* this *is what you did?* some of her predecessors had been asked during their presentations. *You were goofing off at Disney World? What a waste, going so far away, spending all that money—you could have done the same thing here only, no?* She owed it to her family, as well, to do her best. They were paying the balance of her trip's expenses, a significant sum given the rupee-to-dollar conversion, much more than her college fees for the year.

I had no doubt at all, I said, that she'd do marvelously and make the best use of every opportunity here. I wished my own students had a fraction of her focus and drive. Was it true, she asked me, that the American maths syllabus was "low" compared to India's, by which I knew she meant less rigorous? What I'd found to be the biggest difference between the Indian and American systems, I said, was that everyone did not have to study the same things: the curriculum was split into courses, some mandatory and others, like trigonometry and calculus, optional. There was also, as she might expect, less training to answer questions at speed.

I thought of her mother as I said this, my uncle's wife, a mathematics lecturer who conducted private lessons at home for students preparing to take the Boards, those protracted examinations administered simultaneously across the country to millions of tenth and twelfth graders, which I had practiced for with her help, spending a week at their house in Chennai during the month of March, working through fat books of practice questions in the dripping summer heat, under a ceiling fan that stirred the fetid air between power outages. Despite the oppressive weather, I'd been able to concentrate for long stretches, immersed in the broth of that house, steered by my aunt's clear explanations and her kind presence. I never heard her berate my cousin in the extended ways my mother berated me; their interactions seemed all ease and humor and affection. Seeing my cousin now, on her first foray far from home, I suspected that she was eager to explore and experience, but that unlike me, she'd be happy to return when the time came, that wherever else she went in the future, home would always be the place of her childhood.

I was always finding discrepancies, I told her, between the ways we'd been taught in India and how I was supposed to teach here: American students' resistance to memorizing the formulas I still remembered from my high school days, the liberal use of graphing calculators, the pronunciation of "centripetal," "adiabatic," and "corollary."

But you actually want to be a writer, yes? she said with the mix of skepticism and wonder I'd grown to expect from relatives and friends back in India. You're teaching just to make money? For her, writing was quite tough, she added. She'd rather solve a hundred maths problems than write an essay. The way she got by on English exams was to quote long passages from whatever text they were reading. For her Boards she memorized *Hamlet* in its entirety, not just the soliloquies. Everybody knew that the longer your answers were, the higher the marks you got. Her corollary went: the more sentences she regurgitated in the exam hall, the fewer she had to come up with on her own. By the end of the allotted time, as she numbered and stapled her foolscap sheets, she could predict, from the thickness of the stack, whether her score would be in the eighties or nineties. She enjoyed *Hamlet* more than she thought she would, partly because she found the characters somewhat ridiculous. Polonius especially: O, I am slain! She flailed an arm, downed the last of her hot chocolate, and retrieved from her shoulder bag a tasseled muffler, matching hat, and suede gloves. You need proper winter boots, I said, helping to wrap the muffler around her neck. Her mother had knitted it for her, she said, and hearing that made me tie the ends a little more snugly, to make sure it gave her warmth. She insisted her feet felt fine, she was wearing woolen socks, but I suspected those shoes weren't water resistant, that if she stepped into snow, the moisture would seep through the seams. I considered taking her straight to a shoe store—we were in the vicinity of several and it was the season of sales, post-Christmas—but I foresaw awkwardness in the venture. No matter how discounted the boots, they would still be outside her budget, and if I bought them, it would make something shift between us: I'd become an elder, a guardian sort. Perhaps that was what was needed. Let me know, I said to her, if your toes start going numb.

We crossed Tremont Street to the meeting point. Our guide, dressed in nineteenth-century costume, introduced himself as a free Black citizen whose grandmother had been enslaved and whose mother, a cook in the house of a wealthy merchant on Beacon Hill, had borne eight other children, all of whom died of typhus while still young. Puffs of steam billowed from his mouth as he spoke; my cousin turned to me wide eyed—clearly she was impressed, by the story of the character he was playing, I assumed, and the grim histories it embodied, and by his voice, which was startlingly deep and sonorous. I'd explored the Freedom Trail only one other time, when I'd come to interview for the teaching job. I didn't feel like I could afford a paid tour, so I'd followed the trail myself, all the way to Bunker Hill, accompanied by a glossy map I'd picked up at the tourist center.

There were only three others in our group, a man from Toronto and a couple from Wisconsin. We walked to a clearing in the Common, in full view of the State House and its gold dome, and our guide, his long cloak swinging about him, asked each of us where we were from. If my cousin hadn't been with me, I might have said India; I don't know what exactly about her presence prompted me to say Cambridge, some need to highlight for everyone the fact that, unlike her, I hadn't just arrived here. The guide rubbed his hands at my cousin's response. Back then, he said, it would have taken you months and months to sail around the world from India, and when your ship finally docked in the harbor, you'd have smelled beans cooking, hence the name Beantown.

I was reminded that my own home city on the other side of the world also took its name from boiled beans. There must be many other Beantowns, I thought, if in my limited travels I'd already managed to live in two, one landlocked and one coastal. As our guide continued to tell his stories—of these paths being originally trod by cows, of the gold dome having once been wooden until Paul Revere and his sons plated it with copper, of the theft of the wood-carved Sacred Cod by a group of Harvard students, holding up the deliberations of the state legislature for days—I watched my cousin listening with something like rapture, frequently clapping her hand over her mouth in shock and delight. I, too, was engaged by the anecdotes, some of which were even familiar to me, captivated by our guide's delivery. Infotainment, I thought: the thing that had been absent from my own education and that my students expected. None of them would have been particularly impressed by the tour; to find this presentation refreshing, one needed to have been exposed to history, as my cousin and I had, as little more than a compendium of facts to be memorized—the precise dimensions of the Taj Mahal, the number of soldiers killed in the Kalinga War.

We followed him through the Granary Burying Ground and then to Old City Hall, where my cousin gave me her camera to take a picture of her and our guide on either side of the brass donkey. As he pointed across the street to the Omni Parker House hotel and listed the eminent personalities who'd both dined and served food there, she whispered to me that he reminded her of her mother's uncle, who had a reputation in the family for his vibrant retellings of stories from the epics. How is his health? I asked, knowing he'd been diagnosed not so long ago with cancer. She stared at me, and I knew, a moment before she stated it, that he'd died. No one told you? I muttered that I'd forgotten, that indeed my mother had let me know; it was just one of those things that tended to happen when you lived so far from home. I did vaguely remember the email message delivering the news. I must not have fully absorbed it, and the image of her great-uncle from the last time I'd seen him, during one of my trips home from college—his usual gregarious self—hadn't been overridden. I shivered in my coat. The narrow streets funneled the wind in this part of the city, and the shadows of the taller buildings blocked the sun. When we reached the site of the Boston Massacre and gathered around the commemorative plaque in the sidewalk, I saw that my cousin's teeth were chattering. She'd tucked her hands under her arms and was bent over. It's almost done, I told her. We'll get some hot soup.

She nodded, her teeth bared no longer in a smile but a wince. As our guide, ever loud and cheerful, waved us onward, she shook her head. 1770 only, she muttered to me. It's not that long ago. Why do they act like it's ancient history?

It's a young country, I said, but she shrugged in a way that made it clear her excitement had worn off. She was cold and fatigued; I became anxious myself for the tour to end so I could take her indoors somewhere to warm up. This used to be waterfront property, our guide was telling us as we stood outside Faneuil Hall in the wind, the ocean used to be right here; if you go to the Boston Public Library, if you take a stroll through the Public Garden or Back Bay, you're walking on land that didn't exist two hundred years ago. It was the first time I was hearing this, and it gave me a jolt to know that so much of the solid ground of this city—not the buildings and streets, but the earth itself, the very terrain beneath our feet—was a recent phenomenon. The last thing I'm going to point out to you, our guide said, is the golden grasshopper. We followed his pointing arm to the weather vane, lit up in the sun, and when he told us it contained a time capsule, with old coins and writings sealed in its belly, I felt a little lift to think that each time I was in the area and saw the shining fixture, I'd know there was more to it. Happy to give you directions to your next destination if you need, he said in conclusion. I dropped some money in his hat and asked, linking my arm with my cousin's, if he could recommend a pizza place, that my cousin was looking forward, having come all the way from India, to good pizza. He looked at me with incredulity. Didn't you say you're from around here? Best pizza's in the North End, everybody knows *that*, girl.

The North End is an Italian neighborhood, I said to my cousin, loud enough for our guide to hear so he'd know that I wasn't a complete ignoramus. Seeing her glazed eyes and chattering teeth, I added, Let's take a break first, and pulled her toward Quincy Market.

In the food court, she shuffled beside me, stooped, down the central aisle and past the bright stalls that stretched endlessly into the distance. She seemed oblivious to the giant pretzels, rotating gyros, chocolate bars in their glittering wraps, but then, to my relief, she shook herself and made a beeline for a sweets stall. A family friend, she said, had brought some baklava home from Egypt and she'd had a craving for it ever since. We went up to the rotunda, she with her dessert wrapped in waxed paper, me carrying two containers of soup on a tray: clam chowder, tomato. As we sat above the bustling crowd, she flexed her gloved hands, ate a spoonful, and sighed with satisfaction. There'd been a moment outside, she said, when she'd felt as if the cold had penetrated all the way: it was taking her over from both sides, and when the advancing fronts met around her stomach, she'd be frozen solid.

A pity it isn't snowing today, I said. Snowy days tend to be warmer.

She frowned for a moment before her face cleared and she exclaimed triumphantly, as if this were an oral quiz, Latent heat of condensation! Water drops have to release heat in order to freeze. But how can people sleep outside here? she went on, her excitement quickly fading. She'd seen a homeless person on our walk, she said, curled on a bench next to his grocery cart of possessions. There were shelters, I said, but yes, it was unconscionable that a country as rich as this one left their poorest to sleep—and die—in the streets. I could never live here, she said decisively. I'm happy I came, I'm going to make the most of the internship, but I don't want to stay here afterward. Her jaw was set as she tore open a packet of oyster crackers. This is a cold, cruel country, she declared. The weather is cruel, and the society is cruel. Wait till you see the spring, I said. It was beautiful where I'd gone to college, a slightly warmer climate, but with many of the same blossoming trees: cherry, apple, and dogwood. I'd heard that the colors in early spring, like those of fall, were even more dramatic in New England.

She suspected it was beautiful enough, but she didn't want to get used to living here the way too many did. It was good to visit, to see a different part of the world, to avail herself of opportunities we didn't have back home, but it was shameful how few of us returned to make our own country better. Her Quincy uncle had come to America the year she was born. His intent then was to do his PhD and go back, but he ended up staying, first for a postdoc and then for a full-time job at the pharmaceutical company where he now had a senior position in the marketing division; the company had sponsored his green card early on, and he'd acquired American citizenship soon after. What irked her was how he kept saying that at some point he wanted to move back to India, when it was obvious how accustomed he was to his lifestyle here, his salary and the many comforts it afforded him and his wife and two boys, the respect and status he enjoyed at work, the house with two garages, the temple group he was part of, the Indian grocery store a half hour's drive away. Who was he fooling when he said he wanted to go back?

There were lots of people going back these days, I started to say, but she interrupted me. If I meant the techies, then they were ten times worse than her uncle; she wished they would stay in California or Texas or wherever else they settled instead of coming back in droves with their millions, erecting gated neighborhoods complete with gyms and swimming pools and whatever luxuries they'd grown accustomed to here, sending their kids in chauffeured cars to international schools and piano lessons. They claim, she said, to come back so their children can be exposed to traditional Indian values and whatnot, but then they make every effort to isolate them from the discomforts you don't have here. So those kids end up living in these stupid bubbles with others like them—American citizens, basically, since all of them were born here—not even knowing how to cross a regular Indian street. She sneered, and for the first time her face looked ugly to me, the way her lip curled over her bulging teeth. My father has this friend, she said, who moved back to Chennai from San Francisco. We went to visit them, in their "village," as they call it, built on land purchased from the true villagers, farmers who can no longer afford to grow crops because the water table is so depleted. She shuddered as if the cold had followed her inside. What she found particularly satisfying, as she and her mother followed the Bay Area–returned techie around his Indian mansion and listened to him extol its virtues—the gadgets, the architectural design, the lighting—was that she could smell, from over the three-meter compound wall, the stench of sewage. There's nothing he can do about it, she said gleefully. He can build the poshest house he wants, and even closed windows and air purifiers won't keep out the stench, it'll be like a voice screaming at him all the time, *This is India!*

Her shriek of laughter made people at surrounding tables twist their necks to look at us. She shrank in her chair and bit her tongue, still smiling, in that classic Indian expression of sheepishness. To me, I said, the larger tragedy in what she'd just described was the general state of the environment back home—the drought, the pollution. The last time I'd traveled by auto-rickshaw across the city to see a friend, a journey I'd made several times in my childhood without serious consequence—or maybe I just didn't used to notice the dust and exhaust—by the end of the day my lungs felt like they'd been scraped against concrete. The way you describe it, she said, laughing again. Must be because you're a writer, no? She unwrapped her baklava and offered half to me. It would be easier here, she said, than in India, to find other writers with a good command of English. She could see why I'd want to be here. She herself was not good at writing and had never liked big books, she found them intimidating, although *Great Expectations*, which was part of her English syllabus, surprised her once she got past the first few pages. She kept thinking,

This is so boring, so slow, why are they making us read this, what are we learning that's going to be useful in our future lives?—but then around the time that Pip started going to Miss Havisham's, she became interested and still couldn't say why, exactly. It may have been how her teacher spoke about the characters as if they were real people and drew students' attention to details they wouldn't have noticed on their own. Once these things were pointed out, they became easy to follow, fun to follow; it was like finding one's way through a maze, or solving a mystery, even though *Great Expectations* was not a mystery novel. By the end of it, Dickens had become her favorite author.

He could keep you busy for a while, I said.

A commotion made us look down through the railing. Below, in the atrium, a woman was sprawled on the floor, hair spilling from the rim of her coat, a bright-pink bag clutched in one hand. She was lying on her side, her arm, with the bag at the end of it, outstretched behind her, legs apart. A hush spread around us on the balcony as people gazed down. My cousin looked fearfully at me and I felt a moment's irritation. Yes, I thought, it looks serious, but why are you looking at me as if I should know something? As we watched, a figure crouched beside the woman, and the crowd shifted, blocking them from view. My cousin stood up, her hands covering her mouth, looking like she might at any moment scream. Then the crowd shifted again, and the woman reemerged, erect and disheveled, her hand pressed to her head as she was led to a nearby bench. My cousin exhaled. Thank god, she said, sitting back down. She seemed quite shaken, which puzzled me. Growing up in an Indian city, she would have seen all kinds of accidents, close misses, injuries—but perhaps it was the jet lag, I decided, fatigue conspiring with the cold to make her anxious.

We nibbled our baklava in silence, still watching the scene below. Two paramedics had arrived, and the woman, now standing, though a little unsteadily, seemed to be waving them off. The crowd had thinned to a handful of people who seemed reluctant to leave, as if convinced they could still be of help. One person was offering a bottle of water, another what looked like a pastry. The woman stumbled;

the paramedics advanced, and again she resisted them. I was grateful that my cousin did not ask why, because if I'd had to describe how expensive medical care could be in America, her reaction might have left me feeling implicated in the cruelty.

Pizza? I asked, but she was no longer hungry. What would you like to do next?

She smiled shyly at me. Is your place far from here? Can I please see it? I just want to see where you live.

It was barely light anymore. I led the way briskly, almost jogging for my cousin's sake, to help her keep warm, and as if to reward us for our efficiency, a train pulled in just as we were descending the last of the stairs at Downtown Crossing. At the open bridge across the Charles, I tapped the window behind us, and she took in the cityscape, its spangle of lights and their reflections in the water. I moved last week, I said. My old place got damaged in a snowstorm.

Is it bigger? she asked. The new one?

Smaller, I said. Much smaller in fact. But I don't have to share it with anyone, which means it's quieter, and I like that.

If everything went according to plan, she said, she, along with two others, would be renting the apartment that three current interns at her program were soon vacating. She'd seen pictures: a table, chairs, and a stove but no beds, which didn't bother her as she'd never had any trouble sleeping on the floor. When I suggested an air mattress, she made a dismissive sound. I'll be spending a lot of nights at the lab. It's not worth buying furniture.

In the foyer, as I collected my mail from the box, my cousin looked around in approval. They've maintained it well, she said. Very clean. We climbed the stairs, and I wondered why we hadn't planned to meet here. I could have lent her an extra sweater or jacket; we could have walked to Harvard Square and taken a tour there. Less walking, less opportunity to grow cold, and I could have showed her my favorite bookstores. It's small, I said, stepping aside to let her in. She stood in the middle of the room and looked around slowly. This is where you write? she asked, gesturing to the table where my computer sat closed. I put it there to charge, I said. I do most of my writing in that chair by the bay window. She stared at where I was pointing and nodded. Sit now with your laptop, she said. I want to get a photo of you.

Posing for photographs usually embarrassed me, but I readily sat for this one. If she sent it to her parents, and if they then sent it to mine, I wouldn't care; in fact, I hoped it would happen. When I was living at the landlord's mother's, I'd sent a picture of the exterior of the house, and my parents had asked me several times to take some of the room. I'd kept saying I would, I hadn't had time. There, I thought, now you can see.

It's not that small, my cousin was saying as she returned her camera to her bag. When you said small, I was picturing a room half the size. She pointed to the floor alongside the futon couch. I could have slept here. Easily.

CHAPTER TWELVE

Pedro, my downstairs neighbor, accepted the glass of wine I'd poured him. We were in the middle of my apartment, a few feet from the door, which he'd left open on his way in. Neither of us moved to close it, despite the draft from the stairwell; instead, we stood facing each other expectantly, our drinks aloft for what seemed a long time, until finally, laughing, we clinked. Thank you, he said, this is very nice, it's fun to see your place, I've always wondered what the other rooms in the building look like.

I could still hear our glasses ringing—a rich sound, I thought, for such cheap glasses to make. I'd purchased them on my way home from work at Boomerangs, for twenty-five cents apiece, before heading to the liquor store, where I'd selected a bottle whose label called to me: a watercolor sketch of a galloping horse. Pedro took a sip, then swirled his glass, his face an earnest frown. It needs to breathe, he declared, one hand in the pocket of his trousers, which were crisp and, like his button-down checkered shirt, seemed tailored precisely to his measurements. He was almost dainty, brown curls framing a pink-cheeked face, and his gaze, dark and liquid, sent a quiver through me. Your timing was perfect, he said. I was just thinking, It's the middle of the week, a glass of wine would be great, and then you knocked on my door.

I happened to leave work early, I said as casually as I could, so, I thought I'd see if you were free. I didn't mention the incident that afternoon that had put me in a celebratory mood: a student's mother came into the office, walked up to my desk, and told me her daughter was loving my physics class, that I'd become her favorite teacher, the first ever to explain science in a way that made sense to her. I held my breath, waiting for the accusations that I was sure this praise was prelude to, but the mother, a harried-looking woman all in leather, backed away, saying she was in a rush, that she would love to speak with me another time. Amy keeps telling me, she said quickly, Mom, you've got to meet my physics teacher—she's this tiny Indian woman, she speaks English so well, and she's just so *clear* about everything. And as you all know—she waved a gloved hand at Andy, who was looking over from his desk—Amy's a tough customer, right? When the mother left, I turned to him. I don't know what I've been doing differently, I said, and in response he smiled and shrugged. My guess is you've hit your stride and the compliments will keep coming. I tried to return to my grading but couldn't focus, so I took the early train home. It was windy and below freezing, but the cold invigorated me in a way I'd never felt before, as did the bumping and swaying of the train, and by the time I reached Central Square, I knew what I wanted to do.

As Pedro studied his wine again, I opened the slim carton of breadsticks he'd brought. We'd run into each other a few times in the months since I'd moved in, and had at each meeting lingered in the foyer to talk. He was a PhD candidate in anthropology at Harvard; he'd grown up in Colombia and, like me, come to the United States as an undergraduate. His father was a businessman—a wealthy one, I surmised, given Pedro's expensive-looking clothes and the fact that he owned a car, a Volkswagen Beetle. They were from Cardullo's, he'd said of the breadsticks. He took great pride in going to Cardullo's. He went at least every other week and never bought more than one item per visit. It was proof he was resisting the cheap and plentiful junk favored by American capitalism, whose lure he'd succumbed to his freshman year, when, in the giant food court that doubled as his college's dining hall, he'd eaten a cheeseburger, fries, pizza, and ice cream every day of the week. By the end of first semester, he'd gained fifty pounds. You wouldn't have recognized me, he said. I was such a fatty, I had rolls spilling over my belt and a double chin, it was disgusting. He was too embarrassed to ask his father to send money for new clothes, so he lived his entire second semester in sweatpants. He tried working out every day, thinking that he could eat whatever he wanted and just burn it off at the gym, but the more he exercised, the bigger he got, even when he switched his diet entirely, first to salads, and then to smoothies. It was as if America had hacked his body: all it could do was gain weight, he could restrict himself to water or even just air, and his body would find a way of turning it into flab. When he returned home to Bogotá at the end of freshman year, he was a laughingstock—his little sisters couldn't stop poking his belly and puffing out their cheeks. What brought their teasing—and eventually the extra weight—to an end was a stomach bug that his family passed around, which didn't affect him until everybody else had recovered and then made him so violently ill and dehydrated he had to be taken to the hospital and put on a drip. When he went back to Bowdoin, it was not only with a changed body but with a heightened sensitivity to the flavors of food. The smells of a restaurant could be dizzying, and when he ate a few bites of bread, if it was fresh and dipped in good olive oil, he felt satiated completely. I eat more with my nose than my mouth now, he said, twirling his fingers in the air, and I eat with my eyes. That's why I like Cardullo's so much: those beautiful jars and boxes from around the world, places where people pay special attention to beauty and quality and recognize that they shouldn't come cheap.

He sat down on my futon couch and agitated the contents of his wineglass once more. It's starting to open up, he said with his endearing lisp, resting his drink on one knee and looking up at me. Tell me more, he said, about your research.

Research? I asked.

Didn't you say you were a physicist?

Physics teacher.

But you majored in physics, right? Didn't you say you were published in *Nature* or something like that?

No, no, I said, laughing, nothing close. I'd done a research project on cold atoms in college, that was all. I went to the corkboard I'd hung by the window and took down the color printout of my adviser's article that listed me as second author. I made a graph, I told Pedro as he took the pages from me. That was my main contribution. It took me months to learn how to use the apparatus, and once I did, I spent most of my time repairing and adjusting it. There'd been about a month when we couldn't take any measurements because the cloud of cold atoms we were trapping with lasers and a magnetic field—a cloud a fraction of a millimeter across, which appeared as a thumb-sized blot when magnified and videoed by an infrared camera—refused to appear on the screen. It was then, watching my professor and his postdoc work through the setback while I grew more and more frustrated, that I understood I didn't have the deep love of the subject necessary to be a serious researcher.

Tell me about these atoms, Pedro said, leaning forward, still gazing eagerly at me. Why are they cold? Won't the lasers heat them up?

I swallowed more wine and felt my face flush. When an atom is caught in a laser beam, it can be slowed down the way a bowling ball moving one way could be slowed by a torrent of marbles going the other. And since, at a microscopic level, temperature is a measure of the kinetic energy of a group of atoms, the slower they move the colder they are, so to speak.

How cold? Pedro said.

Within a few degrees of absolute zero.

What would happen if your atoms reached it?

They would lose their identity.

I waited for him to ask me what that meant. Instead, he read my full name aloud, slowly, then handed the pages back to me. Beautiful name, he said. Hearing me talk about cold atoms recalled to him that time in his life when he was captivated by physics. At the age of sixteen, he'd spent a week in a daze after reading a book about quantum mechanics. The idea that an electron could be everywhere and nowhere at the same time blew his mind, as did the notion that most of an atom comprised empty space—which meant that everything around and within him was mostly empty space—and this space was actually not empty but full of matter and antimatter spontaneously popping into existence and annihilating each other. How can all this be? he kept asking himself. How can the cat in the box be dead and alive at the same time? How, when I run toward a wall, is there a real chance I'll actually pass through it? Fractals enthralled him, too. This idea of the infinitesimal made sense to him in a way that the uncertainty principle and other esoteric theories didn't. I hope, he said, you won't take this the wrong way: though I find things like black holes and time travel cool, I'm kind of skeptical that they're real.

The bright colors of my bedspread, which I'd pinned to the wall like an unframed painting, lit up the apartment, and went nicely, I noted now, with the clothes I was wearing. Cold atoms, I said, were very much real. They were a state of matter with its own unique properties, like solid, liquid, and gas. A cloud of cold atoms had zero electrical resistance and could slow light to walking speed.

That made no difference, Pedro said. His knees had started to jiggle, and his gaze was fixed no longer on me but on the floor. Things that had been quote, unquote *proven*, he said, still demanded a measure of faith if they didn't make intuitive sense. There was no way any of us could verify for ourselves the hundreds of things claimed as true, so we were at the mercy of reports written by the experts, fact-checked, we're promised, by other experts—all of whom shared the same background and frame of reference that we, on the outside, did not. Our choice was either trust what we were told or adopt an alternative story. Both were dangerous—he knew he could easily concoct a wholly different reality for himself, the way he had as a boy, when he and his friends played pirates and wizards.

But didn't you know it was a fantasy the whole time you were playing?

Of course, he said, but that didn't stop it from exerting a profound influence on him. The balloon of his make-believe world was tethered by just a string. One snip and he'd be off floating. It didn't take very much. His freshman roommate, to this day, floated around in just such a balloon. You wouldn't have any inkling if you watched him from the outside. He was a talented flautist and regular performer at church concerts. He rode his bicycle everywhere, purchased all his clothes secondhand; when he went to a restaurant, he brought his own containers for leftovers. He'd built a composting toilet, he got his food from local farms—in short, he took every step imaginable to reduce his carbon footprint. But he didn't believe in global warming. It was obnoxious, he'd say, for us to think that human beings could have such a big influence on the planet—the reason we should stop using fossil fuels is that they cause wars. He believed 9/11 was an inside job and the moon landing was a hoax. The guy embodied the reasons Pedro had decided to study anthropology. I'm intrigued, he said, by human beings in general and how things like conspiracy theories affect and don't affect human behavior—that's the broad subject of my dissertation.

His legs had stopped jiggling, and he smiled contentedly. It must be interesting for you, he said, rolling the stem of his glass between his fingers, to observe all those students in front of you every day.

It was odd, I said, but when I stood in front of a classroom, I barely saw the students—they became one diffuse, vaguely malevolent organism. But I'd been wondering lately at faculty meetings if teachers, because of their daily, prolonged closeness to kids, were more likely than other adults to behave like teenagers: moody, sarcastic, obstructive. At last week's gathering, one earnest colleague of mine said he couldn't help noticing how many of us seemed to be letting our students out of class early, which meant the kids were wandering the campus at odd times of day. What's your goal? someone retorted. You just want everyone to know you don't let your students leave their desks until the very last minute? Someone else whined, Aren't we overworked already? I give so much of myself to this job, and now I'm being told it's not good enough, I need to be squeezed for every last second of my time—is this the sort of school we want to be, where our colleagues police instead of trust us? Olga, my Russian colleague, had the last word. Different clocks, she said with a yawn, tell different times—simple solution is for someone to go around once a month and make sure they remain synchronized.

Pedro didn't laugh at my imitation of her accent, and I wondered if I'd made a fool of myself. Through the wine-induced ringing in my ears, I heard him say his long-term goal was to work for the United Nations. His uncle, a retired diplomat, would have to put in a word for him if he was to have any chance of being hired—it was impossible to join a UN organization without connections. But once he was in, he would get the UN to sponsor him for a green card.

So, you want to stay here.

Maybe, he said. There were other options. It annoyed him when people acted like there were only two possibilities: the US or where you came from, as if there was no chance he'd want to live somewhere else—Mexico, Europe, Asia—or might not want to stay anywhere for very long. A green card would give him flexibility, he said, and if the six-month residency-period requirement became onerous, he'd consider applying for citizenship, but even that would never make him feel obligated to stay here. Despite its sheer size, the USA felt to him a small place, one where he could come to feel claustrophobic. He attributed this to the small-mindedness and ignorance of its people. That they could rally—twice—behind a buffoon like George W. Bush made him reluctant to claim any connection with this country. He wanted to be a citizen of the world, to feel like he could belong anywhere and nowhere at the same time. He emptied his drink in a single mouthful, grabbed the bottle, and rose to refill my glass first. His cell phone rang as he poured. An old friend, he said, glancing at the phone before sliding it back in his pocket. I'll call her later.

He studied his glass. He'd known her since freshman year, this friend who'd just called, and he was guessing she'd tell him she was getting married. For years now she'd been part of a threesome, and he had no idea which of her two boyfriends it would be. She was equally close to both, and they did everything together: cooked in her tiny

New York apartment, slept in the same bed, took trips, and they'd kept this up for at least three years. Over the past months, she'd called him several times to talk about her feelings—she considered him a brother now, though they'd briefly dated in college—and he'd told her, If you choose one of them, you'll be hurting the other, there's no escaping it. If all three of you are happy, if it's working for you, keep it that way. But she wants stability, security, kids the traditional way, a house with a yard. She wants everything, and I keep telling her, You can't have everything. If you want a man who'll be faithful to you and a good dad, chances are he's not going to be okay with you sleeping with another guy. She's also a bit wild, as you can imagine. He shook his head ruefully and stared into his glass. They'd started dating as sophomores and had been inseparable for a time—couldn't go anywhere or do anything without holding hands. At the end of that year, they'd agreed while on a walk through the woods that their closeness was sealing them off from others at a phase in their lives when they needed to be open to everybody and everything. It was painful for him at the time, but what astonished him now, looking back, was how they'd come together months later as part of a larger group, seven in all, including the two future boyfriends. They went on hiking trips, traveled to Puerto Rico for spring break; in their senior year they'd moved into a large house off campus, where they spent much of every Sunday cooking meals for the entire week and apportioning them into Tupperware containers marked with their initials. It was clear to him that this would be the happiest time of his life, that he would never again feel the same sense of belonging. You must know what I'm talking about, he said, everyone must have experienced this at some point, the feeling of being part of something beautiful, of missing it while it's still happening.

I thought of my own final months in college, how I'd spent a lot of that time, when I wasn't in the science building, alone in my room, soaking in the view from my bay window—of the president's mansion, with its sloping slate roof, and of the willow trees circling the nearby pond, so near but also distant—this view of a world I could never call my own but that I found beautiful and had been granted permission to enjoy for a short while. No, I told him, I'd never been part of a tight-knit group the way he had. I'd spent too much time studying.

Hanging out with your atoms, he said, winking. He wondered if his former girlfriend had found someone new; he suspected that if she'd chosen one of her boyfriends, he would have heard from him—or the other—by now. Unless they were depressed—they both had a tendency toward the disease, and he hoped for their sake they were taking their medications. He gave a start as he said this, then took up his phone again and began to tap at the keys with both thumbs. In his preoccupied state, his mouth hung open in an unsightly way, the edge of his tongue resting wetly against his lower lip. All fine, he said at last, putting the phone away. His friend had just called on a whim to say hi, that was all. She'd recently gone to India, coincidentally—he gestured toward me as he said this—for a meditation retreat.

I finished the last breadstick on the plate. My mouth was dry; the ringing in my ears had turned to a mild dizziness. I worried that if I stood up to fill a glass at the sink, I might stumble.

When she wasn't traveling, he went on, his former girlfriend worked as a waitress in Brooklyn and was studying to be an acupuncturist. You remind me a little of her, he said, leaning toward me. Something about your smile, I think, but I can tell you're also independent, emotionally independent, you have a calm confidence about you. She's always looking for debate. She thinks of herself as a proud Latina and sees me as a confused Colombian. There's no such thing as a world citizen, she used to say, because the role of a citizen is to hold his government to account, and there's no such thing as a world government. I think at some level she believes I don't love my country, which isn't true.

He examined his empty glass before standing up and placing it on the counter. I stood, too, and put a hand on the table to steady myself. I heard him say we should go for a walk one of these days, and maybe to the MFA to see the Ansel Adams exhibit. He was an amateur photographer himself; Adams had always been an inspiration to him. I'd love to go, I said. I helped chaperone a group of students there last weekend. It's part of my teaching contract—chaperoning two weekend activities a year. A student went missing, and I spent most of the time wandering the museum in search of him, only to find, when I returned, that he'd been walking through the exhibit all along; my fellow chaperone had tried to send me a text, but service in that part of the building was so poor it hadn't sent. I'd like nothing better than to go again and focus properly on the photographs.

A floorboard creaked beneath us as he stepped toward me. His hand lifted—I expected him to touch my arm or shoulder, but instead he reached for the back of my head and grasped it tight. When his mouth found mine, I kissed him partly out of gratitude, for in my drunken state I might have fallen if not for his support.

CHAPTER THIRTEEN

On the ride to our hotel, the cabdriver, an Iraqi man, told my colleagues and me that, where he used to live in Michigan, two feet of snowfall in one day was no big deal, unlike here in Seattle, where a tiny storm like this made everyone freak out. He said "no big deal" and "freak out" with an American accent; the rest of his words were labored, as if he was working to separate the English sounds from those of his native language. At the airport he'd sprung out of the car to help load our luggage—a smiling, strong-looking man in a black hoodie and gold wristwatch, who before we'd buckled our seat belts was already telling us he planned to visit Boston soon: he'd heard it was a beautiful city, and his son, who was twelve, had been begging to go to Fenway Park and watch the Red Sox play.

How long have you been in the United States? Raphael asked.

Seven years. I came in 2000.

And how have things been for you?

Good, good, he said. Fine.

People treat you all right?

We were gliding up a ramp to a highway. Large, wet snowflakes spattered the windshield. Sitting in the back seat, flanked by Yuna and Keiko, I could see the driver's face in the rearview mirror. His brow was furrowed, and his eyeglasses reflected the glare of passing streetlamps. Sometimes, he said, I have to tell people I come from

Lebanon or Jordan—I know if I say Iraq they could get angry—but in general American people are good people, kind people.

Really, you still think so? Raphael said. After what our country did to yours? He chuckled at his own question before settling further into the passenger seat, propping his knees against the dashboard and his elbow on the window frame. He and I had never spoken much at work, though I saw him most mornings on the commuter-rail platform at Porter Square, where he liked to stand by himself with a book, his head, with its pile of dreadlocks, towering above the crowd as he swayed and bobbed to the music playing in his earphones. He taught history and coached basketball, and it seemed to me that away from his students, among whom he had a devoted following, he was something of a recluse who would emerge unexpectedly to strike up conversation and then just as suddenly retreat into his cave. He'd approached me only once, back in September, on the train, sliding into the seat beside mine to say he was reading a biography of Mahatma Gandhi and it had made him curious about India in ways he'd never been before. How do Indians view Black people? he asked. My response came out long winded: I said something about how there was deep prejudice against dark skin and, at the same time, Nelson Mandela was a beloved figure, a sign that people felt a natural solidarity with others who'd been colonized, though it was undeniable that there were Indians in Africa who treated their Black servants like slaves—I'd heard this from a family friend who'd spent many years in Kenya—and incidents of violence against domestics were commonplace in India, too.

Would he be safe visiting? Raphael asked.

To be honest, I said, I couldn't say for sure. When I was in high school, a young Nigerian man in my home city, a medical student, was in a motorcycle accident late at night, and the police left him to bleed to death by the side of the road. He was a foreigner, an officer said. If he doesn't know how to drive properly, it's not our problem. Had the student been white, I said, the reaction would have been different, no question. Raphael exhaled with a whistling sound. I tried to reassure myself in the weeks that followed, when he seemed not to want to talk to me again, that he simply preferred to be alone on the train ride, that this was his chance to read and enjoy his music before the clamor of the teaching day, but I couldn't help wondering if I'd failed a test, if he'd been interested not so much in India as in judging, from my answer, the sort of person I was, and that I'd ended up proving to be, along with my country, unlikable. When the train reached Wilton he'd continue to ignore me, adjusting the straps of his backpack and striding rapidly ahead. Perhaps he liked to make a point of walking by himself. It was a legend at the school that he'd been stopped more than once by town police driving by. Are you lost? the police would invariably ask. No, officer, are you? I imagined him answering quietly, in the same slow voice that was now making our cabdriver laugh nervously. He'd left, he said, before things in his country had "gotten really bad." He blamed Saddam more than the Americans.

Yeah, so do Americans, Raphael said.

In the mirror I saw the driver's eyes dart to and fro.

Do you have family back there? Keiko asked, leaning forward.

We'd stopped at a traffic light, having exited the highway onto what looked like a main street lined with shops, many still decorated with Christmas lights. All of his family was here, the driver said. His older brother, a doctor, had emigrated more than ten years ago and had since sponsored green cards for their parents and siblings.

So, do you feel at home here? she asked.

Yes, he said with a deep nod. America is my home.

Do you think you'll always feel that way?

Again the nervous laugh. He looked over his shoulder as he made a left turn. Yes, he said, always.

Keiko sat back and looked at me. On the flight, she'd said feeling at home in America was a luxury for white people, that though she was American herself and had no other place in the world to call home—there was no way she could say she felt *at home* unless she made clear that it didn't mean the same sort of letting one's guard down and being at ease that it did for someone who'd grown up never having to feel like the world around them was a cage, built by people who wanted to keep them separate, who would smile and deny the existence of the cage while constantly reinforcing its bars. Her parents, in their California house, had been awakened in the middle of the night and marched to an internment camp—there was no way the effects of that experience could be erased in one generation. It's been useful, Keiko said, swirling a ginger ale in its plastic airline cup, this inability I have to feel like I ever truly belong. It keeps me prepared. It's odd to me how many colleagues of ours will say without hesitation that the school feels like their *home*, that the staff and faculty and students are like *family* to them. I've been teaching for twenty-five years and not once have I ever thought of my place of work as home. I want to say, Wake up, people, the school is your employer, it's an institution. She rolled her eyes, tossed back the rest of her drink, and reclined her seat. Earlier she'd said she was tired and going to nap, but now she talked on, her voice rising above the engine noise as, behind her, I watched cloud vapors billow and stream over the plane's wing, its distant tip blinking every few moments through the mist. When employees are let go, she continued—laid off, fired, whatever—people act like there's been a mass slaughter. This lady, Dodo we all called her, was in charge of the kitchen—she'd reheat leftover pizza sandwiches and serve them all week until they were so hard you could crack a tooth—finally, after ten years, they kicked her out, and people said, Oh that's so cruel, she was like family. We had a librarian a few years ago from Trinidad who was a disciplinarian and rubbed a lot of people the wrong way. The library functioned right for the first time ever, but the kids found her too harsh, the adults called her standoffish. I saw it coming the first day I met her. I thought, It's a pity, you have so much to offer, and this place just doesn't know how to receive it. When she was fired, those same adults went on about how tragic it was that our school couldn't find and retain people of color. Marie and I were talking about burnout the other day. This is her first year not attending the conference. I asked her why she didn't sign up and she said, I'm so tired and worn out I don't think I can take it, I'm scared that if I go, I won't come back. Speaking of which—Keiko leaned over and grabbed my arm, laughing—you realize, don't you, that ninety percent of the school's diversity is right here on this flight? I mean, if this plane goes down, can you *imagine*?

You're here for a vacation? the cabdriver asked. We'd reached the hotel entrance and were waiting for a line of cars ahead of us to pull up.

We're here for a conference, Keiko said. It's called the Educators of Color Conference. Do you know that term, "person of color"?

Again I saw his eyes dart back and forth and heard his nervous laugh. Then the friendly persona was trotted out again. So, you are all teachers? What subjects do you teach?

I freaked him out, Keiko said once we were in the lobby and the driver had sped away. I totally freaked him out, poor dude, and she laughed and stumbled as we made our way to the reception desk. Her cheeks were flushed, her eyes roving as if it had not been ginger ale on the flight. This was her ninth year at the conference, she said, and the conference was what kept her sane. It was her release valve for all the built-up stress from the things she dearly wished she could say out loud at work but didn't. She was so glad—here she swept her arm toward Yuna and me—she was so glad that the school had finally put its money where its mouth was and paid for more faculty of color to come. It was a small step but in the right direction. She wished she'd had the benefit of this conference as a young teacher—those lonely years full of angst, when she regularly saw and heard things her white colleagues treated as perfectly normal, and had to wonder, Is it me who's crazy? She was bound to get herself into trouble these next few days; she already had a reputation as a rabble-rouser. I call people out, as you know, she said. Sometimes I get really fired up. You guys—she looped one arm through Raphael's and another through Yuna's—you need to keep me in check. Her phone buzzed, and she stopped to look down. Oh, you all go ahead. I'll check in later. Some friends just landed—I want to wait for them here.

Raphael had his own room; Yuna and I were sharing. In the elevator, Yuna asked him what he was looking forward to the most, and he shrugged. Checking out Seattle. Chilling with my buddies. There's a group of about five of us, we'll see each other and catch up over drinks. He shook his head. Don't get me wrong, I think Keiko is fantastic, but she's nuts. She needs to find people close to home, not wait every year for this conference. If you don't have real friends in your life—he threw a sidelong glance at me—then man, it's gotta be rough.

■

Like Raphael, Yuna said, once she and I were in our room and unpacking, she too found Keiko a bit difficult. The first day Keiko had sat across from her in the cafeteria, Yuna felt her spine tingle, as if a snake were in the vicinity. Keiko bent low over her tray, eyes flashing: So you're the one, was her opening line. After all these years, the school finally hired another Asian. Yuna thought, Oof, this is what it's going to be like, I know this type—intense, charismatic, confiding, I'll find myself getting close to her, and before you know it something I say will set her off and her fangs will come out—but we're going to have no choice but to be allies in this place because we're the only Asians.

She paused to look at me. Sorry, she said. I meant East Asian obviously.

No need to explain, I said. In my first semester of college, a fellow student had told me with a straight face, You're not really Asian, and at the time I thought this was a reflection of Americans' poor knowledge of world geography—so I joked that yes, a long, long time ago, India had been an island, and then it collided with the Eurasian Plate and formed the Himalayas—but since then, to the best of my knowledge, it had been part of the continent of Asia, which meant that being Indian made me Asian, yes? Well, you don't look like this—my fellow student had pushed up the outer corners of her eyes. In America when we say Asian, that's basically what we mean.

Yuna leaned against the bathroom door and waved her toothbrush in the air like a conductor. And what we say as white Americans, she said, what we white Americans declare to be Asian shall be so, because we want our sushi and our Chinese takeout and our bibimbap to be served to us by people who look the part. She put her fingers to the outer corners of her eyes. Her first husband, who was white, used to tease her this way. Whenever she was angry at him, he'd mimic her by stretching his eyes with his fingers and opening his mouth wide. This is what you look like, he'd say, and instantly she'd retreat, ashamed, for she'd been told throughout childhood, by her teachers and parents, that she had a nasty temper and would have to learn to control it. Her husband seemed, when she met him in college, the first person in the world to find her instantly likable. He in turn had grown up with an abusive father whose rages made him allergic to displays of anger and desirous of affection, which Yuna was happy to shower on him. Whenever I overhear a couple talking baby talk with each other, I cringe, she said. It's what he and I did all the time. Like we were reliving our childhoods and reparenting each other. It worked fine for six years. Then I had a miscarriage and could no longer do the baby talk.

My phone buzzed with a text message. It was Pedro.

You're smiling, Yuna told me.

A guy I'm getting to know, I said.

With a wink she went back into the bathroom and closed the door.

The moment after I replied to Pedro's text, my battery gave out, and I realized, after rummaging through my suitcase, that I'd forgotten to pack a charger. Yuna's phone and mine were different models. When she came out, wrapped in a bath towel, she suggested I call the reception desk to ask if they had a spare.

I'll do it in a while, I said, and she looked at me, surprised. He's working on a paper, just wanted to know I'd arrived safely.

Yuna sat down on her bed, facing me, still wrapped in her towel. How serious are you about this guy?

We'd been on one proper date so far, I said.

And?

He'd taken me to the Museum of Fine Arts. I hadn't expected the day to go well because little things seemed to upset him on the drive over, starting, as we got into his car, with the bird shit on his windshield. The birds always picked his car, he said, wherever he parked. Even when it wasn't under a tree, they seemed to have it in for him. He opened the passenger door and ushered me in like a good valet. Then I heard him rummaging in the trunk, and he reappeared by the driver's-side window with a rag and a spray bottle. He wet the cloth, set the bottle on the hood, and scrubbed at his defiled windshield, clutching at the rag with both hands. He was sweating by the time he started the engine, which he revved a few times as if to scare away any lingering birds. Behind the wheel, he was erratic, swerving around vehicles and then sighing in exasperation when the inevitable chorus of honks followed. Pedestrians triggered a similar reaction. I get it, they need space, he said after braking sharply for a woman in a crosswalk. But they don't need to act like they own the road. I was concerned his moodiness would follow us into the museum, but as soon as he parked, he pronounced that he was no longer stressed out, that driving always made him so, but now that we were at his favorite place in Boston, he'd be able, in his words, to be himself again. I was struck by how familiar he was with the building, the way he led me through galleries and hallways, around corners, without ever consulting a map or the signage on the walls, straight to the artifacts he wanted to show me. We started with the mummies, then moved to the blue-and-white porcelain bowls from China. In the Impressionist wing, he gave me a tip about how to look at a painting: close one eye and stand a little off center—I suspected, I told Yuna, that this would be old hat to many people, but for me, who'd never had artistic training, it was a revelation: the painter closes one eye to make objects collapse into lines, so then when you the observer look at the canvas without a second eye to remind you of its flatness, the marks transform like a pop-up book into those same hills and trees that faced the holder of the brush. I lingered, squinting, before the Monets and the Van Goghs, until Pedro whispered in my ear, Just checking, we have another hour until the place closes, do you still want to see Ansel Adams? I apologized for keeping him waiting, but he was happy, he insisted, very happy I was enjoying myself. The Adams exhibit was in a separate wing; we held hands on our way there, and once we reached the gallery, we spent a lot of time kissing in front of the silver prints.

Good choice, Yuna said. Adams was an exception for her when it came to photography, especially black-and-white landscape photography, which she tended to find sentimental and manipulative. His birch forests made her quake.

For me it was the still life with the boiled egg and slicer that set me quaking, the way the strings, taut and metallic, were touching, no, resting, on that damp, white flesh, reveling, it seemed, in their power to hover there, with no rush to plunge. Pedro said it was the egg waiting, eager to be cut—he could sense its anticipation, it was pushing upward, ready for the strings to run it through. Needless to say, we kissed for a long time before the egg.

Yuna gazed at me with her chin cupped in her hands. Her bare legs wound glamorously around each other below the hem of her towel. I sensed her suppressing something—an opinion or piece of advice, and this made me say with some emphasis that, although I found Pedro attractive, I was still very much getting to know him. Our apartments were stacked one over the other, which made it awkward at times, like the morning when he'd told me he wouldn't be home later, he had a department meeting that would go at least till 8:00 p.m., but then that evening I heard him downstairs, talking on the phone, letting the refrigerator door slam. I thought of knocking and saying casually, Hi, you're home! But it seemed like an aggressive move. I wished we weren't living in the same building. It seemed essential, when you were getting to know another person, to see just a little of them at a time, the parts of their lives they wanted you to see, let them control how much they showed. When we ran into each other the next day, I asked about his meeting, keeping my voice casual, and he said, with no hesitation, that it had gone fine.

Was there a chance, Yuna asked, that the meeting had been rescheduled?

The point, I said, was that his meetings were none of my business and I didn't want to come across as nosy. I hated nosiness—it reminded me of the Indian aunties who made it their business to know everything about everyone.

Yuna studied me with narrowed eyes and a puckered mouth. It seems to me, she said, that you're expecting him to disappoint you.

What I was really feeling at that moment, though I didn't say so, was pleasure. In Pedro's last text before my phone died, he said he was missing me. It was his first such declaration since our kisses at the museum and I wanted to inhale the thrill of it—and the added thrill of making him wait for my reply.

■

Walking through Pike Place the next day with three Indian women, I saw how people's glances took in the four of us together and was reminded of the keynote speaker's address that morning, when he'd spread his hands and said in hushed tones, to whistles and applause: I was lying in bed picturing all of us flying through the snow, from all corners of the country, descending here, and I thought, Man, Seattle's getting darker, it's getting darker by the minute.

We strolled past the florists and fishmongers, down a brick-paved alley flanked by restaurants. Curbstones glistened with dampness; melted snow dribbled from awnings and wet the shoulders of our jackets. One of my companions, Akhila, was telling us about her recent engagement, an arranged match, whose cancellation a week earlier, caused by her own realization that she couldn't go through with it, had prompted her to register for the conference. This is the first time I've ever signed up for something that bills itself as exclusively for non-whites, she said as we settled ourselves in a small Thai café, at a table overseen by a life-size seated Buddha carved from wood. A waiter brought us water in narrow glasses, and after we ordered, Akhila said she was feeling calmer now, there had been a moment during our affinity group when she was afraid she might collapse, so overwhelming was the experience of being surrounded by people who looked and spoke like her and whom she could speak to without needing to explain herself that something, some muscle she'd never realized was clenching, had let go too quickly. I'm not used to losing control, she said, smoothing her palms over the tasseled green scarf that was wound and knotted around her neck. The backs of her hands were patterned intricately with henna, a vestige, I assumed, of the engagement ceremony. She was in her midthirties, big breasted, with a wide, smooth face and elongated eyes set so close together they seemed to have sprouted like leaves from the stem of her nose. Her woolen dress, a size too small, was cinched tightly at the waist by a leather belt, and she held herself rigidly straight in her chair. Her father, she went on, could never abide the term "people of color." "Colored" to him was the white man's word for people like us, and when he said white man, he meant British. We Indians are the superior ones, he was constantly reminding his children, with our ancient culture, our music, our food, our language, we're ten times more sophisticated than the Westerners. They are the real barbarians, and it's when we accept their characterization of us as coolies, darkies, coloreds, whatever, that we dig our own graves. For him, the whole point of coming to America was to get away from what he saw as his country's inferiority complex. He arrived in the sixties, a time when Indian engineers and doctors were being handed green cards as soon as they stepped off the plane. America is nothing without us, he liked to proclaim. So please don't ever get into the habit of saying we're colored people or oppressed people or nonsense like that.

I never did get into such a habit, Akhila said, because at some level I must have seen myself as white—or if not white, then at least not conspicuously brown. I grew up in this sheltered suburb of Houston where at school everybody dressed the same, talked the same, acted the same—it was a monoculture of affluence. I remember when we sang "Ten Little Indians" in second grade, how I looked around to see if anyone was looking at me. Nobody was, and this made me stand a little prouder and sing with all my might. I didn't know the song wasn't actually about people like me: I hung on to that private joy of knowing I was different but didn't stand out. My favorite dolls were blue-eyed blondes; sometimes I drew bindis on them but that's about as far as I went. It's not like I was isolated from my family's culture: my mother cooked traditional food all the time, we socialized with other Punjabi families, went to Delhi every few years to visit relatives and attend weddings. I enjoyed it all but from a distance, like it was not me exactly but my avatar, my ancestral avatar, wearing a sari and speaking Punjabi and dancing to bhangra music. All my crushes in high school were white boys, so I assumed I'd eventually marry one. Until, and I'm still trying to figure out how I let it happen, my parents introduced me to an Indian guy and I came this close—she pinched her thumb and index finger together—this close to going through with it.

For me it was the opposite, Lakshmi said merrily. Younger than Akhila, she had the coiled energy of a dancer and a broad, easy grin. I knew growing up that there was no way, no way in hell I'd ever marry either a white guy or an Indian guy. One represented oppression, the other familiarity, and what I was after was freedom and difference. Until I met my husband, of course, who's half Indian, half white—so only somewhat oppressive and somewhat boring.

She laughed at herself in a way that made it easy to imagine her presence in the classroom: lively, charismatic, self-deprecating. Across the table, Sonal, the oldest of our group, shook her head solemnly. If she ever had a type, she said, it was the mummy's boy: gentle, goofy, narcissistic. All the men she'd dated postcollege fit this mold. She'd developed her cooking skills taking care of them. They were happy to eat her dinners, happy to let her fold their clothes and bring them beer or chai as they lounged in front of the television, and for the first several months of each relationship, she considered any word of thanks an adequate expression of their love, but then, slowly, cracks of resentment would invade her feelings, and one day out of the blue she'd start raging at these men she'd chosen to share her time with.

Sonal stared into her lap as she spoke, her voice so soft it was barely audible, her ears protruding, gnomelike, from under a frizzy mop of hair streaked with gray. She knew now, she said, where her rage came from. Her father used to treat her mother like a servant.

He left for work at dawn; when he came home at night, he'd take off his shoes and tie, roll up his shirtsleeves, and eat, without a word of acknowledgment, the full Indian meal—dals, curries, rice, chapatis, popadams—that had taken her the greater part of the day to prepare. He never so much as bought her a bouquet of flowers for her birthday, and if she ever asked him to book a vacation somewhere or take them out to a restaurant for dinner, he'd claim they didn't have the money for such frivolities. Raging at him was useless—he'd tell her she was acting like a child—so she vented her frustration on Sonal and her sister. Any little thing we missed, like not putting our shoes on the rack, she'd fly off the handle. Tell us we had no heart, that we thought she was dirt, that we made her want to run back to India. We'd leave stuff around and act out just to provoke her—it was horribly satisfying to see her, this adult who was supposed to be in charge of us, throw a temper tantrum. As a teenager, I was resolved never to have an arranged match: clearly my mother was miserable because she'd been forced to marry a man she couldn't love, a man who brought her to this country to be nothing more than a housewife and mother. But then I was suddenly forty, still unpartnered, and feeling my life was slipping away fast.

With fingers that trembled, she peeled the paper sleeve off a straw. Our teas had arrived, bright-orange infusions swirling with milk. For a time, Sonal said, she'd contemplated being single for the rest of her life and wondered if that would really be such a bad thing, given that she was one of those teachers who knew of no other way to do the job than to give herself over completely to her students. Their needs preoccupied her during the school year, and in the summer, she tended a large and prolific vegetable patch in a community garden. Taking care of things is second nature to me, she said. So finally I told my parents, If you still want to arrange for me to meet an Indian guy, find me someone who understands that I have this insatiable urge to give and look after, that I do it altruistically with my students and my plants, and so I need someone who will do the same for me: someone who is willing to cook for me and clean up after me and go out of their way to make sure my needs are met—find me a househusband, and my parents said, in unison, without even looking at each other, Have you gone mad?

She giggled, an unexpectedly girlish sound, rolled her tired eyes, and sipped her tea through her straw. Our waiter was placing food before us: bowls with colorful, shimmering curries garnished with orchid blossoms. So I guess I was lucky, Sonal went on, I didn't have to go through the whole matchmaking saga because my parents decided I was a hopeless case for thinking, even for a moment, that any self-respecting Indian man would be a househusband. I'm still living alone, but I have a friend, a lover you might say, one of my fellow gardeners. My parents know him and they've given up asking me what our intentions are. She lifted a hand and placed it on Akhila's shoulder. Getting older helps, makes it easier to do your own thing.

Akhila was chewing with her eyes closed, holding a napkin over her mouth, struggling apparently with some emotion.

You don't have to talk about it, Lakshmi said earnestly.

Akhila's leaflike eyes, now watery, opened as the napkin came down. I'm fine, she said. I should have told the waiter, Yes, I know I'm Indian, but please, no chilis, my spice tolerance is zero. She smiled, her rigid face and body relaxing a little. The reason she'd consented to let her parents find her a match was that the guy she'd considered "the one," a mathematics teacher from Greece whom she'd met online— they'd been a couple for well over a year and were talking about getting an apartment together—had out of the blue announced in a text message that he was breaking up with her and returning to Greece. It was the biggest shock she'd ever suffered in her life: the waves of grief and confusion that it triggered lasted weeks and then months. I can't trust myself to ever again find someone on my own, she'd thought, and so gave her parents the go-ahead. They wasted no time activating their networks, and within days an astrologer had been consulted and a meeting arranged in Houston between the families. She tried to tell herself the whole point of the exercise was precisely not to know her partner beforehand, to commit first and figure it all out later.

He's a good man, she tried to tell herself, with a good, stable career, he checks all the boxes, our horoscopes align, this is how it's been done for centuries, I've tried other routes and they've failed, so why not take this one and trust it will work? But in their conversations—about five in total if you counted the first one in the presence of both families—the more she tried to see him as her life partner, the more her impulses kept screaming no, until finally, one day before the engagement ceremony, she wrote an email to him, cc'ing her parents and his, to say she couldn't go through with it.

Her gaze fixed on her lunch plate as if she were checking the recesses of memory for any neglected detail. As a teenager, she said, she spent a lot of time at the house of a friend of hers, her best friend. Each time she visited, she saw a bouquet in a vase on the dining table, and her friend would say, Those are just I-love-you flowers my dad brought for my mom. Years later it came out that he'd been carrying on a long-term affair—he'd buy flowers for his wife on his way home from his mistress's house. Akhila still couldn't shake the conviction that the bouquet symbolized an unshakable adoration, the sort she must crave and had never been able to find. She sighed and served herself a spoonful of plain rice. Carbs, she said, passing the bowl. I have to watch out for them. She moved her palms down the sides of her body, over her tight dress.

It could well have been, Lakshmi said, resting her cheek against her hand, her smile less carefree than before, that your friend's father loved his wife even as he was deceiving her. She knew someone in San Francisco, a woman from the same coastal community in Kerala as her, who was devoted to her husband and for decades had a weekly standing date with another man, a colleague who lived in an apartment overlooking the Golden Gate Bridge. It was a good balance—the colleague gave her what her husband couldn't, so he allowed the woman to be happy and not hold any grudges against her husband—who was, it had to be said, a good but not exactly attractive man. In the town where they'd both grown up, she, the daughter of a fisherman, was a local beauty, and he, fat and lame in both legs from polio, was the only son of a merchant navy captain. He proposed when she was sixteen, saying he'd provide for her, make it possible for her to go anywhere in the world, pursue any field of study—and she, wanting to be a fashion designer and model, agreed. By now she'd retired from modeling, but she was still thin and gorgeous, while he'd grown bald and increasingly fat and lame. I visited their house in California, Lakshmi said, and it was clear to me from the way he looked at her that he worshipped her, but it was also clear, from how she listened and talked to him, gently, with no hint of contempt, that she loved him as well. Deeply. I wouldn't be surprised if he knows about her infidelity, though she claims he doesn't. There's not a huge Malayali community in the San Francisco area, unlike, say, in Dubai, so I guess part of what keeps them together is that they come from the same place.

I asked Lakshmi if she spoke Malayalam, and she said that while she could understand it quite well, her relatives always laughed to hear her speak it. She'd been to India many times and found it fascinating that people there, strangers on the street, were able to tell that she was American. She could wear a salwar kameez or a sari, she could be completely silent so no one would hear her accent, but it was like people had a sixth sense—they would come up to her in shops, at tourist spots, and say, You're from America, no? It's your complexion, a cousin told her. Your skin looks fresh. If you lived here, the sun and the pollution would make it darker and drier. It's everything about you, another cousin said. Your mannerisms, your walk, your posture, the way you nod, the way you smile—it's obvious you're not from here even if you look like us. And of course, in America she was used to being asked if she was African, Brazilian, Caribbean. The reason she'd tried not to date white guys was that they made her feel like a white girl in brown skin. And I could tell I made them feel safe, she said, safe and good about themselves: my girlfriend is a person of color, how can I be racist? When I start listing to my husband the ways in which he benefits from his whiteness, he always says at some point, I've taken on about as much white guilt as one half-white guy can take on, seriously.

She turned to me, laughing. Do we seem really old to you? I can tell from your face that you're thinking, No way my love life is going to be anywhere near as complicated.

Don't make assumptions, Sonal said. All three women were now looking at me with amusement. She could be dating five guys at once for all we know. Oh, look, she's blushing. Tell us, is he a desi?

Colombian, I said, and we've only been dating a few weeks.

Sonal's weathered face lit up, and she shook back her silver-streaked hair. She loved Latin men, she said, making a fanning motion with her hand. In her experience, they really did seem to have it in their blood to dance. She used to take salsa and mariachi classes; there'd been a period in her late twenties, early thirties, when she'd been a regular at a dance club. More than the Sanskrit and bharatanatyam lessons her parents had subjected her to, it was salsa that made her feel most in touch with her Indian roots—its sensuality, the way the steps embraced the natural swing of her hips. She'd had to learn to shed the stiffness of the good Indian girl she'd been raised to be— modest, quiet, demure—and channel the deeper layers of her history: the mesmerizing voluptuousness of temple figurines; the Kama Sutra, which she'd read as part of a sociology class in college, taught by an Indian professor who called the book the world's first sex-ed manual. It's hard to believe, she said, when she thought of her mother's and grandmother's stern demeanors and their squeamishness around all things sexual, that their ancestors enjoyed elaborate tantric orgies, that even their more recent foremothers had walked around with their breasts free, no bras, no blouses, their bodies draped loosely with saris, before the British came along and imposed their Victorian notions of modesty.

Has he taken you dancing? Akhila asked me as she served herself another small spoonful of rice.

I'm not sure he likes to dance.

You're sure he's Colombian?

Oh, stop it, Lakshmi told her before reaching over and taking my wrist, her wide grin restored. You and he are both foreigners, she said reassuringly. It means you have that commonality of experience. Before Tim and I got married, I dreamed of dating someone from outside America and India, someone from Portugal, say, or Morocco, who spoke a different language and cooked yummy food from some exotic culture and had family in a place I'd have fun visiting—it would feel like a proper vacation.

I thought about that morning's conversation with Pedro: he'd picked up on the first ring and said my name in a way I'd never heard him say it before. It made my skin tingle. He missed the sound of my feet above his ceiling and the prospect of opening his door to see me on the way in or out. It was almost more fun, he said, to run into me by chance than to make plans. My energy infused the place; something felt off when I wasn't there. I haven't cooked for you yet, he said. I'll make you my specialty: lasagna. Not exactly Colombian, he acknowledged, but his Italian friends pronounced his version to be excellent.

You're smiling again, Lakshmi said, her fingers still encircling my wrist.

He's funny sometimes, I said, my Colombian dude.

If you're laughing at his jokes, she said, that's a good sign. You seem a serious sort. He could either complement you well or drive you crazy. It all depends on the sort of chemistry you have.

Does he like Indian food? Akhila said. That would be an important question for me. She set down her fork, pushed away her half-empty plate, and planted her plump elbows on the table, all signs of stiffness gone as she spread her fingers, with their shapely, painted nails, in a gesture of wonderment. If you two can't go to an Indian restaurant together, then what's the point?

I said I myself had yet to visit an Indian restaurant in America that I liked.

I get you, Lakshmi said, releasing my wrist. I get you one hundred percent. Her voice rose, and she thumped the table with her fist. Most Indian places suck. I'll tell you why they suck. It's because Americans have this narrow, rigid idea of what constitutes Indian cuisine, and Indian restaurants keep pandering to it. She had a cousin, a professionally trained chef, who'd tried to open an upscale restaurant in Los Angeles and discovered just how difficult it was to expand the American palate. Her cousin sourced spices from individual estates in Kerala, her signature dish was a fish stew that took two full days to prepare, and when she priced it at thirty-five dollars, people claimed it was too expensive: the same white folks who had no trouble paying fifty or more for some oozing dish at a fancy French restaurant, but who couldn't conceive of Indian food being anything but cheap. Her cousin, after being forced to close the restaurant, retreated to catering in hopes that there would be weddings and other occasions where she could showcase her best dishes, which married the spices and cooking methods of Kerala with the local ingredients of California—an expression, in other words, of her true self. Selves. But there was no getting away from demands for the usual naan and raita and chicken tikka masala.

So what happened to her? Akhila asked.

She married a wealthy guy, Lakshmi said, shrugging. A superwealthy guy, actually. They throw lavish parties for which she doesn't prepare a single thing. If she steps into the kitchen, it's to press a button for espresso.

It seemed strange, I said, that her cousin no longer wanted to cook. I'd imagined her as an artist, someone with a passion, who, once the stresses of having to make ends meet were removed, would feel a newfound freedom to create.

My companions exchanged glances in a way that suggested my statement struck them as rather droll. Our bill arrived, and as we dropped our credit cards into the tray, Akhila thanked us solemnly. This was the medicine she'd needed, she considered us family and hoped we'd stay in touch. If we were ever in Chicago and needed a place to crash, her apartment was open to us. Or my mansion, she said, if I'm as fortunate as Lakshmi's cousin, in which case, believe me—she raised a finger toward me—you will *not* find me working.

◼

It wasn't until the final day of the conference that I was able to spend more time with Indu, who at our first meeting had given me her card and said, of her full name, I've forgotten how to pronounce it, I've lived here too long. She looked me up and down and added wistfully, You remind me of myself when I was your age. Which flattered me, for I'd been contemplating her as someone I would want to look like when I was old enough to have wrinkles and gray hair, features she made no attempt to conceal. She was in her sixties, slender and stately looking. Her attire, haircut, and jewelry all struck me as impeccably tasteful, an effortless, subtle balance of East and West. Earlier, during a brief address to the conference as a member of its board, she'd spoken about her experience as the first South Asian principal of a California high school, and I'd flinched each time she made a mistake—a stammer here and there, an error in syntax, a bewildered look in her eyes when she glanced up from her notes, as if she'd forgotten for a moment the character she was playing or the audience she was addressing—lapses that were so minor they may not have even registered for most but that threatened the image I wanted the crowd to have: an enviable, outstanding example of someone like me.

Let me ask you something, she said as we took the hotel elevator up to the top floor. At your school, are you the one expected to organize something for Diwali?

I'd been asked to, I said. "Invited" was how the principal had put it, but when she said that it might be too much for me in my first year of teaching, I'd agreed. I suspected I wouldn't be able to get out of it next year.

Indu looked at the floor and slowly shook her elegant head. I can't believe, she said, that this is still happening in 2007. If I were you, I would tell your principal, There are other Indian festivals. Why don't we do Holi for a change, or Ganesh Chaturthi?

I told her that organizing events was not my forte, and she took my elbow in a reassuring manner. Oh, I'm sure that's not true.

In the atrium, we sat at the bar overlooking the city: skyscrapers giving way to ocean. Outside the shut doors of the adjoining auditorium, where closing speeches were scheduled to begin in an hour, waitstaff were stacking cups and saucers on makeshift tables. So, you're an aspiring writer, Indu said. It's strange, but in my lifetime of reading and teaching students how to love literature, I've never had the urge to write a story myself. Except maybe once. My first husband died unexpectedly when our daughter was in primary school—and there was this period of about a year when my parents set me up with eligible men, a string of them, spaced no more than a month apart. They would come to our home for dinner—I was living in Pune with my parents at the time—and my mother would make elaborate meals, we'd all sit around and eat, she and my father would watch the poor fellow critically, how he spoke to my daughter, how he answered questions. I remember my father taking out a notepad and scribbling furiously as his ice cream melted in front of him. Then the stranger and I would have to sit in the living room and converse on our own while my parents put Niki to sleep and cleaned up. They were scared for me, of course, panicked, that I was a widow with this small child, they saw it as essential that I remarry before I turned thirty-five—this was the magic number in my mother's head, the age when a woman transforms overnight into an old hag. There must have been at least ten of these dates, if you can call them that. Each one felt more like a cross between a job interview and the sort of superficial conversation you'd have with the person sitting next to you on a flight—and I've thought, looking back on that year, how it could be interesting to tell the story as just one evening, with all the men blurring together, and me, this harried, full-time teacher and single parent trying to seem young and lighthearted. She shook her head and sighed. When she looked up again, her eyes, beautifully round and dark, were brimming with tears. At some point, she said, I realized I needed a complete change of scene, so that's when I came to Berkeley. I loved the Bay Area instantly. I thought, No wonder everybody wants to come to America, it's so gorgeous. My daughter was nine then. She found her feet quickly, all things considered. Do you mind if I ask, are you planning to have children? It's never too soon to think about, you know. Fertility does decline.

She said this with a grimace, and for an instant her sophistication gave way to something else, something earthier. The next moment her elegance retuned: holding aloft the laminated drink menu, she said, A glass of wine? and waved to the bartender. A young woman with short flaxen braids nodded in our direction as she continued to towel-dry the glass in her hand. She seemed in no hurry to approach, and I wondered if she felt entitled to make a pair of brown women wait. The previous night I'd gone barhopping with a group of conference attendees, and at around one o'clock, as we gathered by the curb for a ride back to the hotel, three taxis in a row slowed down in front of us before speeding away. Finally a pale-skinned, small-built woman stepped forward and raised her hand, and as if on cue a cab pulled up.

The bartender put away the towel and came around, her yellow braids bobbing. Indu ordered a carafe of the Bordeaux, and the server said, smiling, as she collected our menus, that she'd be right back with some fresh rolls and butter.

Some water, too, please, Indu said and turned to me. Have you had a good time?

I told her I'd enjoyed many of the talks, especially the one earlier today by the Native American psychologist. I'd forgotten the violence of the Grimm version of "Cinderella": one stepsister slicing off her big toe, the other cutting off her heel, in order to squeeze their bloody stumps into the glass slipper. I found it thought-provoking that he concluded with the question of what parts of ourselves we slice off in order to fit into a society. It reminded me of an article I'd read about a type of eye surgery in Korea, where the skin of the upper lid is pinched and sutured into a permanent crease to make the eye look more Western. There were equivalent surgeries for the nose and chin, surgeries that young girls signed up for or that were scheduled for them as birthday or graduation gifts. If two candidates with identical résumés made it to the final round of a job interview, went the prevailing view among young women in Seoul, the one with the more Western face would have an advantage. It was sobering, too, to think of the less invasive ways we modified ourselves—our mannerisms, speech, ways of thinking—whether we intended to or not, so we could belong, though I doubted that being aware of what we were giving up or changing would make us less inclined to fit in. I also felt a lingering apprehension about the whole premise of the conference. Perhaps it was the title itself I objected to, as if someone had put a baggage tag around my neck. Had I been asked, I'm sure I would have thought of all kinds of other ways I'd rather be identified, but I also knew I didn't have a choice, that this was who I was in the eyes of the world—of America at least—and there was no getting around it. Still, if I started wondering whether such and such a person was treating me a particular way because of the color of my skin, I'd go crazy, I'd be affected the way a professor of mine had said she was affected by reading Dostoyevsky: when she went out, she felt suspicious of every person she encountered.

Indu laughed, then shook her head at me, smiling. I hope, she said, you didn't find our affinity group off-putting. I don't know if you're aware, but this is the first year we had our own dedicated Indian group instead of being lumped in with the Pakistanis and Sri Lankans. I remember a time when it used to be a pan-Asian affair. In those years the conference used to have white people too—Educators of Color and Their Allies was our title then. About half the attendees were white, and their ignorance drove the rest of us mad. I refuse to be called white, I remember this teacher, an Englishwoman, saying one year, I refuse to categorize myself and others, I don't care if a person is black or blue or green, this race stuff is an American obsession, if you ask me, can't we all just acknowledge that we're of the *human* race? And then she went on about how in England she'd grown up surrounded by immigrants, how her best friend in university was from Bangladesh, how she'd raised her children to love food from all over the world, spicy food especially, how this conference was trying to make her feel that her way of seeing people as *people* was somehow wrong, and what did it say about the world that *categorizing* people, the very thing we were supposed to have learned not to do, was suddenly the thing to do? At the time I'd had some of these same qualms myself—they're inevitable for immigrants to the West if they never had to think of themselves as Black or brown or yellow in their own native contexts. But listening to this white Englishwoman talk, I felt a double flash of anger—toward her and myself. I'd been teaching for something like fifteen years then, mostly in India, teaching Dickens, Twain, Shelley, Scott—writers I'd fallen in love with as a teenager and who I believed were objectively good. They just happened to be white, I'd have said. Watching that Englishwoman carrying on, I saw just how much it benefited her to have me believe what I believed then, and I understood for the first time what a perversion it was for someone like me to make arguments that bolstered the worldview of someone like her.

The flaxen-haired bartender reappeared with our wine, water, and bread. She poured the contents of the carafe into two stemmed glasses, her profile highlighted against the blue sky of the window behind us. Mount Rainier rose in the distance, its white slopes tapering into matching clouds. Can I interest you in some food? she asked brightly.

We're pressed for time, sadly, Indu said, and the bartender, still smiling, assured us she'd be right around if we happened to change our minds.

I don't know if I mentioned to you, Indu said after she'd sampled the wine, that my daughter is a writer. A published writer, it's fair to say.

I retrieved a pen to jot down her daughter's name.

She doesn't have that many publications, Indu said. Some magazine stories on organic farming, and short fiction in a journal that's now out of print. She's been working on a book for the past twenty years. Once she finishes it, she claims, it will bring in enough money to make up for her meager earnings and lack of reliable employment. Indu traced the rim of her wineglass with the tip of her finger, first one way and then the other. I hope, she said, you won't take this as discouragement, but I think it's a good thing, a very good thing, that you have a teaching career for stability. Her daughter was still recovering from a series of setbacks that had culminated in her moving back home, to her childhood room, where it now seemed she might remain indefinitely, with no prospect of a career or financial independence. It was the sort of crisis Indu had been anticipating for decades, ever since the two of them moved to California in the wake of her first husband's death. Everything seemed too good to be true at first: the ease of adjustment, the friendliness of the community in Oakland, the temperate climate—she'd always felt there was something terrible waiting around a corner, that Niki would get into trouble at school, or fail a class, or fall ill with an incurable disease— some calamity would befall them that clearly had something to do with the child losing her father at such a young age. But no such incident happened. Niki was a calm sort of girl, reserved, never at the top of her class but never by any means a bad student. It's true, Indu said, there was a time—a very brief time—when I used to chide her for not working harder, when my instincts as an Indian mom may have gotten the better of me, but I gave all of that up by the time she was a teenager. It was clear that the only effect of my scolding would be to drive her away, and that terrified me because it would leave me all alone. But now look what's happened. She's living in my house, with my husband and me—my forty-one-year-old, able-bodied, intelligent daughter. She couldn't be closer to me if she tried. And yet sometimes I feel as alone and distant from her as if we were on separate planets. I wish it weren't so. I wish she were living a full and happy life, striking out on her own, the way you seem to be doing. I can imagine your parents are proud of you even as they miss you. You talk to them often, I hope.

As often as I can, I said, knowing my mother would disagree, for whenever I did call or email, she chided me for not calling or writing more. I'd let her know that I'd be going to Seattle for a teachers' conference but hadn't mentioned its title for if I had, she would've said she didn't think such characterizations existed in America of all places, and that if indeed they did, then why on earth did I want to stay there?

Indu took a swig of wine and wiped a drop from her lip with her finger. In her speeches as school principal, she said, she regularly encouraged her listeners to follow their dreams. But she marveled that no one had ever challenged such advice, when now her own daughter had become a cautionary tale of what happens when one follows one's dreams and discovers them to be just that: fleeting and ever shifting. At this point her daughter had attended more than eight colleges without completing a basic degree; she'd been an organic farmer, a paralegal, a wilderness guide, an EMT, an ESL teacher, a real estate broker, a waitress, and, most recently, to Indu's consternation, for her daughter had a certain love of drink, a bartender.

She looked morosely into her wineglass before draining it. Remembering those blind dates my parents set me up with, she said, I think of how one's children can remain one's responsibility indefinitely. She cleared her throat, a phlegmy sound, and squinted at me as if her eyes were giving her trouble. Has your mother visited you in Boston?

My parents had come to Pennsylvania for my college graduation, I said, but had not visited since. I imagined that the distance between us, if I chose to stay in America, would become a challenge when they were old and needed help, but at the moment I enjoyed being far away.

When my daughter was in college, Indu said, it dismayed me how infrequently she called, and only when she wanted something— money usually.

I'd never asked my parents for money, I said at once. In college my scholarship covered my tuition, room, and board. Whatever cash

I needed to buy books and other necessities I earned from on-campus jobs.

Indu laughed wearily. We never know when we may need our parents' help, she said. But it's obvious that your mother has raised you to be responsible. Grounded. You're not someone who lives in dreamland. She lifted her empty glass. To your mother.

CHAPTER FOURTEEN

My colleague Stephanie let me know as we drove to work together—
I'd missed my train and called her from the station to ask for a lift—
that she and her boyfriend had gotten engaged. The proposal had
taken her by surprise, she said. He'd been moody and pensive for
days but wouldn't say what was bothering him, which had made her
think the obvious: that he was preparing to dump her. They were out
hiking during spring break, up a hill they'd been planning for months
to climb, and as they were catching their breath on the windy summit,
her now fiancé reached into his backpack and produced a dusty old
box, which she immediately assumed contained something she'd left
at his place—lip balm or a pair of earrings—that he'd brought along
to return to her before announcing it was time to part ways. I want to
tell you something, he'd said shakily, and she'd replied, Fuck you.

He was lifting the lid, she told me, and you should have seen the
devastation on his face, poor guy. She hunched over the steering
wheel, her shoulders shaking with laughter. On her finger was a large
diamond set in gold. The prospect of marriage seemed to have dis-
pelled some of her austereness: she was dressed not in her usual black
but in jeans and a baggy sweater. Her hair, no longer tied back, was
hanging loose, cropped to the base of her neck in damp waves. Cars
honked from behind. We were inching along Fresh Pond Parkway.
The clouds were various shades of charcoal, and against them new

leaves stood out like points of green light. My head ached from a lack of sleep; through the fog of my thoughts, I heard her go on about wedding plans. The date was set for Columbus Day of the following year. We decided to have it in Albany, she said. That's where Brad's from, and his uncle has an estate we can use. She described its acreage, the facilities, and the hotels nearby that could be reserved for guests. They agreed, she and Brad did, about the need to be modest, but modest wasn't the same as cheap. She'd been to several weddings recently and concluded that some things really showed if you took shortcuts. A college friend of hers had had a whole bunch of people over to her dad's ramshackle farmhouse in Vermont, where they spent the night before her wedding baking sourdough bread, fifty loaves of it, in a makeshift oven that made the barn feel like an inferno. And then for the ceremony they strung up this tent in the woods and had all the guests bring a dish to share. Which meant that there were about twenty variations of tabbouleh. Everybody was eaten alive by the bugs, needless to say. Another couple she knew got married at the Crane Estate, one of the most expensive venues in New England and, in her estimation, vastly overrated, despite the spectacular views, especially since, three years on, the couple was getting divorced. She wanted it classy but not extravagant, unpretentious but not shoddy. There were cultures, she knew, where extravagance was acceptable, even required, at weddings. She'd once shared an elevator with an Indian bride who was decked out in so much gold, she looked like a walking sun. Not something Stephanie could ever pull off, but she found it stunning to watch.

She glanced at me, then back at the road. How large is a typical Indian wedding?

I said an invitation in India would typically read: To Mr. and Mrs. So-and-So and their family and friends.

Oh god, she said.

We were passing a long stretch of bare earth colonized by daffodils. My head throbbed, and I wished I could get out and take a walk in the breeze, through those cliques of yellow flowers bobbing like they were deep in gossip. Stephanie asked me if I'd done anything fun over break, and I replied that I'd been to a concert the previous evening. Zakir Hussain.

What does she play?

I didn't feel like correcting her or explaining what the tabla was. An ensemble, I said, playing Hindustani music.

She looked over her shoulder as she changed lanes. We were on I-95, heading past the pond that, ten days earlier, on the last day of winter term, had been covered with sheets of ice knit loosely like the plates of a skull. Now it was an expanse of gray water, its surface too choppy to reflect the surrounding office complexes, which until late October had been concealed by foliage, and then when the leaves fell emerged all at once, slabs of steel and glass stacked crookedly like a child's building blocks.

Did you go alone? she asked.

I went with Pedro.

Oh, the guy in your building? Her voice brightened. How did it go?

I wasn't sure what to say. I'd spent most of the night lying awake thinking about it: the concert, our dinner, the things he'd said and what I'd taken them to mean. A week earlier, when I offered to get tickets, I was surprised by the degree of his enthusiasm. He'd dreamed of seeing the great Hussain live—ever since finding the album *Shakti* as a teenager. He'd once seen a protégé of Zakir's. He hadn't known it was possible for a percussionist's hands—human hands—to move as fast as that drummer's did. Like a hummingbird's wings. Listening, he felt as if he were galloping; his skin started to vibrate. At some point he realized he was holding his breath, that the music had flooded him like water.

We'd agreed to leave by five o'clock and take the T to Symphony Hall. When we stepped out, I braced against the wind—the previous day had been warm enough for short sleeves, but now the cold struck me like something solid. I should have gone back in to get my padded jacket; if I had, the evening might have gone differently. But in the moment, and after the hour I'd spent choosing an outfit, I felt compelled to pretend the sharp breeze was nothing. As we waited on Prospect Street for the lights to change, Pedro complimented me on my raw-silk scarf. It lit up my face, he said, standing back to observe me. He looked relaxed in his heavy coat and wool beret as I told him, shivering, that my mother had had the scarf stitched from material left over from a shirt made for my grandfather, that despite the rising demand for readymade clothes in India, it was still possible to get things sewed there. Most of the clothes I wore growing up were tailored from the lengths of cotton my mother bought in bulk and had made into curtains and tablecloths, which meant I blended into the landscape of my house like a kudu in tall grass. But it was even more embarrassing to go to clothing stores for things like dresses and jeans, because the shop assistants would tell my mother they had nothing in my size; I was too fat.

Hard to imagine, Pedro said, laughing. You're so slender now. And that dress is gorgeous on you. He put an arm around my shoulders. I was grateful for his warmth. The compliments, too. I'd agonized, wanting to wear something Indian for the concert but not so traditional that I'd stand out.

We rode the T to Hynes, then walked through a merciless wind. Once we were in the concert hall, my numbed cheeks and toes started burning; my ears rang. I was still shivering when we got to our seats. Pedro was surprised there wasn't more of a crowd. This was Boston, and hello, thousands of people knew Zakir Hussain. Whoever the organizers were, they'd done a poor job advertising the event; how could one of the world's great musicians, arguably the greatest percussionist, come to a city like ours and not fill even half an auditorium? Let's move down, he whispered as the lights dimmed, and he seized my hand. I whispered to him to wait—I'd slipped off my shoes to finally flex and wriggle my chilled toes—and as he yanked me out of the seat, I tripped and wrenched my ankle. The preperformance announcements had begun, silence all electronics, note the fire exits. He had let go of my hand the instant I stumbled—maybe assuming I'd bent to retrieve my handbag—and moved swiftly to the aisle without looking back. He doesn't care, I thought, rage rising in me. I limped after him to the second row from the balcony railing, where we sidled our way to the middle. We can see so much more, he whispered excitedly, as the musicians, five of them, trooped across the stage and up onto a U-shaped dais. Hussain was at the center, with his curly mop that recalled for me advertisements for Taj Mahal tea, those commercials on Doordarshan where he drummed with the monument in the backdrop and his head of curls, still dark then, thrashing like a tornado. Silently now, he and his compatriots joined hands and bowed, then sat cross-legged. The sitar player began—a solo at first. People were still filing in, many talking as if they had no idea a concert was in progress; the sound system projected the music in a way that made it easy to ignore the surrounding din. I closed my eyes and began to feel calmer. The raga evoked for me the mood of evening: a slow settling at the end of a busy day. When I opened my eyes, Pedro was leaning sideways, tapping the shoulder of a man one row ahead who had his camera out, a small one, with its lit screen facing us. Pedro objected fiercely, and the man lowered the device. What the hell, he murmured to me. There's another guy over there taking pictures, too. And why are they still letting people in?

The flow had swelled. We watched people press in noisily through all the doors as the musicians played. They'd begun at six thirty; it was now past seven. Were the tickets printed wrong or something? Pedro whispered.

Indian Standard Time, I whispered back. He looked at me quizzically, and I shrugged. What could I say? Punctuality was not something my countrypeople were known for. Neither was silence at concerts, since traditionally, before concert halls, performances tended to be outdoor events, at temples, lasting hours and hours, with people free to come and go as they pleased. Where did these people all come from? I wondered now. Were there really so many of us in Boston?

Excuse me, these are our seats.

A couple, both lavishly dressed in silks and chiffon, were hovering beside us. We stood and joined the noisy shuffle up the aisle. A woman in front of us laughed into her phone, and Pedro tapped her shoulder. This is a concert, he hissed.

She brushed him off impatiently and continued her conversation, in Hindi mixed with English, a lingo I didn't speak myself though I could follow along. It reminded me of the Indian Students' Association gatherings at college—loud, Bollywood-inspired parties that I always left wondering why I'd attended in the first place, when I didn't care for Bollywood music or for the tepid, doughy samosas in pans of aluminum foil, and when the people I ended up talking to, people I knew personally and even considered friends, surrounded me with lowbrow banter that I was dismayed to find myself joining in on, as if they—we—reinforced our basest selves in a group.

As Pedro and I threaded our way to our old seats, the ustad bellowed from the stage, drumming: Some people have come to enjoy the music. If you're not one of those, at least let others listen in peace.

There was a smattering of applause and approving grunts, and I hung my head, mortified that my people needed to be talked to this way and that the maestro's admonishment was lost on the crowds still pouring in: whole families with small kids and elderly grandparents, young professionals snapping photographs with their cameras and phones.

It's so disrespectful, Pedro said, shaking his head. This could never happen in Bogotá.

Zakir addressed us again, this time calmly. You see, it's like an Indian highway. In America your roads have steady, predictable frequencies, but in India we'll have Ganesha walking—he drummed a slow, ponderous beat—and a lorry there—his compatriot made a thrumming sound on the ghatam—and cars and rickshaws and motorbikes, and every now and then—his hands blurred in a frenetic pitter-patter—you'll have a boy dashing across on his bicycle.

I glanced at Pedro and was relieved to see him chuckling. Later, at the taqueria where we stopped for dinner, he said he wished he hadn't given up the piano when he was ten, that his decision to abandon his lessons—which he blamed on his teacher, a stern, joyless old woman who told him each week, whether he practiced or not, that he, like the others of his generation, was irresponsible and arrogant—led him to experience concerts as a semiliterate encountering a grand text. It was clear that all the musicians we'd just seen were masters of their instruments, world class. He wished he had access to just a sliver of their understanding; had his music teacher played him some of what we'd heard tonight and said, *This* is what you'll be able to appreciate, there are so many patterns here, shapes within shapes, and even if you can never play them yourself, you'll be able to recognize them the way a true stargazer can recognize constellations and planets, he would have stuck with it.

Unless, he added, the rules of Indian music are totally different.

I wouldn't know, I said as I tried to gather a soft taco around an avalanche of toppings. Having never studied Western music, the most obvious difference I was aware of was that Indian music, like our ancient stories, was passed down orally and never transcribed.

Pedro's eyes widened as he chewed. That makes sense, he said. I was watching them playing so fast, and I was thinking, It's like they're having a conversation, each time they play this piece it will probably sound slightly different, they're improvising, making things up, it's an exercise that relies on listening more than reading. Oh, I love it. He wiped his fingers on a napkin, sat back, and said, I wish I knew more.

I considered explaining what a raga was. But I expected that as soon as I started describing technicalities, he'd ask questions that I wouldn't, with my limited musical knowledge, be able to answer. So instead I said that the sequence they'd played at the end made me feel opposite things in equal measure. I associated with childhood the sense it raised in me of anticipation mixed with disappointment, a premonition almost, as if I knew that as soon as I started looking forward to something my very act of expectation would keep it from materializing. As soon as I tried to assume the worst, to make the favorable outcome a reality, the rules would shift again. When the sitar, sarod, and violin dropped out, leaving the percussionists to do their rounds, their repetitions and deviations, the way they chased one another over hills and valleys, setting each other challenges, sometimes inviting, sometimes taunting, the whole thing became a study in chaos and order, with the overall shape recognizable, but the moment to moment all frenzy.

An Indian highway, Pedro said. He laughed and put his feet on the chair beside me. I scooped salsa with a corn chip. The restaurant was warm. Outside, the wind from earlier had died down. My ankle felt less stiff but still hurt.

I think I'd find India fascinating, he said, but also a bit scary.

Why scary?

From the way people were behaving in the hall, it seemed a bit, how do you say it, barbaric?

The chip scratched my throat on the way down. *Barbaric*.

Crowds, heat, poverty, he went on, none of that stuff turned him off, but lack of respect toward elders and the accomplished, toward a living genius, an obvious prodigy, he couldn't stand. It exposed the true soul of a people, in his opinion. He prided himself on being open and flexible, and as a student of anthropology he tried to be aware, constantly, of the framework that he brought to his way of seeing the world. Growing up in Colombia meant he placed a high value on respect. His lifetime goal had always been to travel the world, but after seeing the way people were behaving in that hall, he wasn't particularly eager to go to India.

Then don't come, I said. We don't want you.

A tremor passed over his face, leaving his mouth slack. He licked his lips, the same lips I'd kissed in the wind on our walk to the T, which now struck me as absurdly pink. And as I straightened my scarf and pulled on my meager coat, he said, weakly, I didn't mean—I wasn't saying anything about *you*.

I stood up, and my ankle, which I'd told him nothing of, briefly gave way. I managed to retrieve my wallet from my bag and count out cash for my meal before telling him I regretted bringing him, that the whole thing had been a waste. I paused before saying the last word, then shouted it at him before departing, moving as briskly as

I could. I limped down Mass Ave. for several minutes before realizing I'd turned the wrong way. I was sweating with pain and shivering from the cold, and when I saw Pedro hurrying toward me, I was relieved to stop.

You hurt your leg?

We faced each other in front of a broken bench. I'm sorry, he said. It never occurred to him I might see his criticisms of the crowd as applying to me. But obviously, he continued, clapping a hand to his chest, obviously you think I insulted your country, yes? I'm sorry. I treated you, like me, as a citizen of the world. People talk about Colombia as if everybody there is a drug dealer, and I just think, Yeah, that's an inaccurate portrayal, but I know the reasons for it, and I'm not going to take any of it personally. I know who *I* am. He clapped his chest again. But obviously, he said, gesturing at me with his other hand, others identify more personally with their home countries, and I totally respect that.

His eyes were wide and pleading; my foot ached, and I let him take my arm. On the train he made one final reference to the concert: while it seemed at first that all but the two of us had their phones out and were talking, really it was probably half or a third of the crowd, and within that there was most likely a subset of a few people who were the root cause of the macro behavior. There was a term for it in social anthropology: submergence, when people lose their sense of individual self and responsibility and end up imitating the bad actions of others.

I wondered why I felt upset at him for criticizing the same behaviors I had scorned, too. In the foyer, I told him, I'm sorry, I may have overreacted.

It's okay, he said, and for some reason his cheeriness brought an echo of the rage I'd felt earlier. Go rest your foot, he said.

I should have dressed more warmly and I twisted my ankle, I told Stephanie as we passed the mud-spattered ENTERING WILTON sign on the highway. But other than that, it was fine.

CHAPTER FIFTEEN

Andy, my department chair, proposed that, unless the heat was too much for me, we step out and find a shady spot on the quadrangle. He didn't expect our conversation to go longer than twenty minutes. And he was joking, he added, about the heat—he knew I was accustomed to hot weather.

I said where I came from in India, summers were hot but never humid like here on the East Coast.

Really? he said. I'd have thought the monsoons would make the whole subcontinent humid. We were still standing across from each other at his desk, and he was searching through piles for what I assumed were documents pertaining to my end-of-year performance review. Until that morning, I'd felt some reassurance, thinking of the compliments he and others had extended to me lately about my teaching and its effect on students, that my job was secure, but now, watching him thumb through a sheaf of papers, his brow furrowed in concentration, I was having doubts.

Bangalore was at an elevation, I said with fake cheerfulness, three thousand feet above sea level, that made the climate relatively mild and arid. The British had favored the place for their barracks, parade grounds, bungalows, and parks. In fact, the cantonment area, as it was still called, remained its own city within a city, where English was spoken more than Kannada and the streets had British names.

Ah, those Brits, Andy said with a chuckle, they leave their mark. As we walked together down the stairs, he said his goal was to acclimate early this year to the heat and humidity, to see if he could make it through the summer without air-conditioning. A cousin had done a similar experiment the previous winter: starting in November, she'd lowered her thermostat by a degree every week to teach her body to adapt to the cold. By March, the temperature in her house was in the forties and she claimed she was perfectly comfortable in no more than a sweatshirt. Inspirational, he'd thought, this is exactly what everybody needs to be doing, this is as much a no-brainer as hybrid cars and efficient light bulbs. But then he visited his cousin in March, the first time they'd seen each other in a year. She'd lost so much flesh—this woman who wasn't fat to begin with—that she'd wrinkled like a deflated balloon. As they sat in a restaurant by a drafty window, Andy kept his coat on while she wrapped ice cubes in her napkin and pressed them to the back of her neck. It's too hot, she kept saying, it's way too hot, people need to realize we can't keep living this way, and when she got up on her chair, a skeleton in clothes, and shouted for the heat to be turned down, it was clear she was in a state of suffering. He tried to reason with her: Phoebe, there's no point in saving the planet if it means losing your humanity. And she shot back: We've lost our humanity already, that's the reason the planet's dying—a response he found so overwhelming in its pessimism he had to excuse himself from their lunch date.

Man, it's hot, he said now, as we sat down at a picnic table in the sun. I barely registered the warmth through my nervous shivering. When I was your age, he said, and in the Peace Corps, I got terrible heatstroke in Kenya. I was teaching English and helping build houses—a real privilege, I've always thought, for an American boy to go to an African village and make a small difference in people's lives. They were so welcoming, the locals, that I must have felt like I was one of them when I went on a long walk in the heat. My friend Eliud ended up having to drive me to a hospital in Nairobi. We'll see how long I last out here.

He pushed up his shirtsleeves, revealing forearms that were paler than his hands, and liver spotted. Well, you've made it to the end, almost, of your first year, and my guess is you've learned by now that teaching is a profession where you give so endlessly of yourself that by June you're a shadow of what you were in September. I used to have a recurring dream of turning around from the blackboard and seeing my students transformed into vampires: black robed, fanged, glassy eyed. The transformation didn't surprise me at all; in my dream I just turned back to the board and went on about acids and bases. When I got home in the evening, my children took one look at me and fled, screaming. I think the dream reflected my fear that my son and daughter might turn from me in resentment because I had so little to give at the end of each day, having exhausted the best of my humor and patience on other people's children, who, as you know, reliably leave us depleted.

But back to your review, he said. I believe in transparency and clear communication, so let's get straight to the point. Congratulations on making it to the end. That's no easy task for anyone, but for someone like you, the adjustment is no doubt harder. I was thinking today about how, when I first started teaching here, Raphael was the sole faculty member of color. Now we have at least seven, and I like to think I played some role in making that happen. It wasn't easy, let me tell you. People have this knee-jerk resistance to change. Why can't we just keep it simple? I've heard folks say. Why can't we just hire the best candidates and admit the best students? A few years ago, at my urging, we paid a consultant to lead a discussion among the faculty. I remember her asking, How do you determine the best candidate or student? and the overwhelming response being something along the lines of: We know it when we see it, they're just a good fit. And then, when she asked how it was that our school had a clear history of hiring people from a particular group, you should have seen the reaction—it was as if she'd accused us of being mass murderers. I have an adopted daughter and she's Black, someone said, as if that somehow answered the question. I don't see my colleagues as white, someone else said, I see them as human beings. You don't hear things like that quite as often anymore. I'm the first to say we have a long way to go, but I remember last year, when you came to interview, thinking you'd have had a very different reception four or even three years earlier. Two other candidates were considered for your position, both, shall we say, a more natural fit for us. But I argued—and people agreed—that we'd do well to give you a chance, that you'd bring something unusual and interesting.

He nodded somberly, as if he were waiting for me to thank him for giving me a chance. Then I realized his somber expression might mean that my fears were about to be confirmed: he was preparing to say I'd disappointed him and the school, that my contract was not going to be renewed, which meant I'd have to leave the country. For good.

I've been thinking lately, Andy went on, and I'd love to hear your opinion on this, I've been thinking that this issue of diversity is really nothing more than expanding the idea of a good fit. Sometimes it's obvious when someone's just not going to work—we hired a vice principal a few years ago who was an out-and-out disciplinarian. He'd go around banging the cafeteria tables at the end of recess and yelling to the kids to get to class. You can imagine that didn't go down well. Another year we had this English teacher with a PhD who took enormous offense when kids criticized the texts she assigned. Little philistines, she called them. Her student evaluations were terrible; there was just no way the school could have renewed her contract. But back to you—well, to be honest, at the start of the year, I feared you were going to take a similar trajectory. Are you a good fit for us permanently? His gaze finally met mine over the rim of his spectacles. I held my breath and waited as his sideburns shifted in the breeze. It's too soon to say for sure, but we're going to give you another year. Ah, here comes Lila.

I let out my breath and turned to see her advancing toward us across the lawn, her rings flashing in the sun as she fanned herself with a manila folder. Ugh, she said in greeting. Her sleeveless blouse, of a layered, ruffled material, was stained with perspiration, and her sallow face was ruddy. This weather, ugh. Even with the new air conditioner in my office, this humidity just gets to me. My daughter-in-law from India—she gestured to me with the folder—says where her grandmother lives the temperature goes into the hundreds every day for weeks. I can't imagine it, I simply can't imagine living there. I'd melt like a candle. I don't care what they say about all humans sharing ninety-nine point whatever percent of our DNA, there's no way I'm built to survive the heat like you are, honey.

She sat beside Andy, her breathing loud and labored, and turned to him. They got rid of Suzanne, she whispered fiercely. Did you know? Just like that, Marissa decided Latin was no longer important, just like that she called in Suzanne and said she'd get no contract for next year. Sorry, your program's been eliminated. Instead of Latin, *Latin*, that's been taught at this school since, well, since the beginning, from now on we're going to have—she bounced her hands off the sides of her head—*Mandarin*!

We're a small school, Andy said wearily. We have to meet changing demands on a tight budget.

Changing demands. Lila snorted. What next? Will we start teaching communist literature because there's a demand for it? I'm all for a welcoming attitude, don't get me wrong, I'm all for being inclusive. I just don't want us becoming, you know, *unrecognizable*. At lunch the other day, I overheard Yuna, no, it was Keiko, saying, For an Eastern language to rise, a Western language must fall—and sniggering as she said it. I thought, Oh, so this is what it's going to be. War! She brought her fists down on the table with a bang that set the loose, freckled flesh of her arms shaking.

Andy cleared his throat and asked if we were all up to date with my paperwork.

Lila opened the folder, still glowering. Let's see, I checked with the lawyers and they said the application to extend your OPT through the end of summer was accepted. So, given that our petition on your behalf was successful and that you already have an H-1B interview appointment at a US consulate in your own country, you should be set to travel home in August. You'll be receiving a Notice of Action letter in the mail confirming your visa extension—make sure you carry that with you. That was your question, right—if your travel dates of August tenth to twentieth would be okay? She sighed, as if my question had caused her an onerous amount of work.

That doesn't give you a whole lot of time with your family, does it? Andy said. Or maybe, he added with a wink, that's the whole point?

Actually, I told them, I'd be spending five weeks, starting in July, at an artists' retreat in Maine.

Andy's shaggy eyebrows lifted in surprise. Congratulations, he said. Is this something you applied for?

Telling Andy the details made me feel again the thrill of opening my acceptance note, which had arrived over the weekend. I'd seen an advertisement back in January, I said, and sent an application. It was a shock to have been selected—I imagined many of the people applying were vastly more accomplished and experienced than I was.

And how much does it cost, if you don't mind my asking?

It's free, I said, except for travel to and from. The retreat accommodated about eight writers at a time. We'd each have a room of our own in a large building with a central kitchen, where we were expected to assemble our own breakfasts and lunches. Dinner was a communal affair, prepared by a chef, and the only real requirement was that we all dine together every evening after a day spent in solitude on our respective projects.

Maine's beautiful, Lila said sharply. But I wouldn't go there in summertime—the bugs are out of control.

Congratulations, Andy said again. Well deserved. Truly. I had no idea you were a writer. He coughed. When he spoke again, his voice had a roughness I'd never heard in it before. Back when I was your age, I rode a motorcycle across the country—I'd love to do that again. It was a dream of mine to travel the world on my bike, keep a diary, with pictures, get it published one day as a book. My first several years teaching, I kept telling myself, I'll do this for another year, and then I'll quit, I'll do this for just one more year. Will you be offended if I offer some advice? Don't do what I did. Don't keep staying if there's something else calling to you.

He looked at me and nodded several times, his lips pressed together as if he didn't trust himself to say more.

My phone buzzed in my pocket, and I stepped away to answer. Did something happen? the landlord's voice said in my ear. Last I heard, you were planning to rent until September at least.

My plans had changed, I said. I'd be moving out the first week of July, but I'd pay rent through August, as promised.

Where are you moving to? Not that it's my business, but I ran into Pedro this morning and he said he hadn't seen much of you lately. I put two and two together, I'm good at this sort of thing. I thought immediately: lovers' quarrel. Happens every year, in at least one of my buildings. Either people get together and then say they're moving out because they need a larger place for the two of them, or they break up and then one of them needs to move out because they can't stand being around each other. It keeps the turnover brisk. I like to tell myself it gives me the chance to keep meeting new people. We were talking in my discussion group about this question of home, what it means to different people, and I almost called you to say, Come join us at Bukowski. A Haitian woman at our meeting said, I don't have the privilege of being able to say, My home is here or my home is there, because home implies that I can walk in whenever I want, without fear of being turned away or questioned or arrested or killed. And my friend Jo asked her, But pardon me, you're a citizen—don't you consider the United States your home? Or at least one of your homes? I thought it was an innocent enough question, but the woman seemed to find it insulting. When you look like me, she said, you can try to tell yourself every day, This country is my home, I belong here, but each time you try to believe that, you will see and hear a hundred things that contradict it. Do you feel the same? the landlord asked me.

I'm not a citizen, I said. Not even a permanent resident.

Right, he said. I'd forgotten. You haven't been here that long. You always seem so self-assured. Any chance you want to move into another place of mine? I have an apartment on Broadway available in September.

Thanks but no, I said. I had found, through the same online forum that had brought me to him, an attractive room in a large apartment near Davis Square.

He chuckled and wished me luck with my new roommates. When I turned back to the picnic table, it was empty, the sun having chased my colleagues indoors.

PART IV

CHAPTER SIXTEEN

Mosquitoes, yes, they are bad, Claudine said as I scratched the fresh bites on my neck, but you are lucky, very lucky, that you didn't come in the month of May, because then there are the blackflies. Horrible, terrible, ferocious animals. She gave an exaggerated shudder. With her breathy voice, her dark, tight clothes, and her vivid makeup— strokes of purple, green, and blue so bright I wondered if she dabbed pigment on her face from the same palette she used for her canvases— she looked about to stride onstage before a packed audience. We do not have them in France, these blackflies, so I was not prepared. When I came here a few years ago, they attacked me, and my whole body became covered in, how do you say it, balls? She tapped her index finger along the length of her arm.

Welts, the poet standing near us said. It was Friday, the weekly cocktail hour, and we, all eight residents, had come to the veranda of the mansion where during the day we spent our time in separate rooms. Mine was down a hallway from Claudine's, at the back of the building, and faced a stretch of wetlands—vast, convoluted shapes of mud and water that I pictured teeming the way stagnant pools teemed during the monsoons in India, mosquitoes and their larvae roiling and surging. The veranda was at the front entrance, above a rose garden, in the center of which a mossy stone dolphin stood upright on its tail fin and exhaled a vertical stream of water. The estate had been built in the late 1800s by a shipping tycoon whose vast fortune his sons had gone on to squander. When the arts foundation took over the mansion and grounds, they replaced the tycoon's name with that of the wetlands, a name that in the language of the local Native tribe meant, simply, "muddy waters." I love the sound of it, don't you? the woman who'd given me a tour when I arrived said, smiling. The sunlight from the window turned her blond hair white, and as she moved through my room to point out a framed architectural plan of the mansion, her stilettos rang sharply against the oak floors. Reminds me always that this is not just a manor, but a *place*, a piece of nature we need to do our best to keep wild.

Welts, Claudine repeated. If you want, she said to me, I can give you some oils. Citronella, geranium, lavender. I brought them all in my carry-on luggage, little bottles, so security check would not be a problem. A drop here, here, here—she tapped her wrists and the backs of her ears—and the insects will not bite.

The poet, Bradley, laughed. Oh yes they will. The horseflies especially. They'll think, Mmm, a little geranium seasoning, chomp chomp. And don't forget the ticks. At an earlier meeting he'd said he was here to finish a book, but since then, I'd always seen him dressed in heavy laced boots, a wide-brimmed hat, and a backpack over one shoulder, as if he'd just returned from a hike or was setting out on one. He now retrieved from the backpack a metal spray can with an orange top. If you want to keep the buggers off, you'll need the real deal. He uncapped it and depressed the nozzle. A spray of droplets settled like dew on the thick hair along his arms as a smell of gasoline wafted our way. This was a special formulation, he said, offering us the can, developed by a chemist friend of his, not available at any store and probably not legal, technically. Claudine, who had been waving her hand in front of her nose, declined through her teeth, which made him shrug and place his offering on a nearby table, among half-drunk wine and beer bottles, their labels soggy with condensation. He had been out walking in the meadows, he said, and came back to find something like two dozen ticks crawling over him. Thanks to the spray, not a single one managed to latch on. Had he resorted to the old herbal repellants—he used to be an *au natural* type of guy, he said, no processed foods, no synthetic bug sprays, no supplements, no drugs— he'd be dealing with multiple cases of embedment.

Oh, I've had lots of ticks, another resident, Miguel, said, having approached the snacks table to retrieve his beer. My girlfriend and I check each other in the evenings—it's a ritual, it's fun. He shrugged, a tall man with a mohawk and multiple ear piercings. A bit of alcohol does the trick if they've latched on.

I'm allergic to meat, Bradley said. All because of a tick bite. Can't drink milk, either.

He looked at Claudine as he spoke. *Allergic?* she said, and he nodded vigorously.

Oh man, Miguel said, I've heard of this. He turned to Claudine. Don't worry, you won't find that species of tick here.

They're migrating, Bradley said loudly. In fact, one of the ticks I pulled from my shorts today had the telltale white dot.

Miguel, taking a swig of beer, looked skeptical. It's a long way from here to Texas. Unless you're saying these insects are carried by the wind, the way sands from the Sahara blow into Europe.

Deer migrate, Bradley said, planting his boots further apart, his hands on his hips. All you need is for this thing to get transmitted from one herd to another every few years. He turned to Claudine again, angling his body as if to block Miguel's view of her. Funny you were asking how this allergy came about. I've been writing a sestina titled "Lone Star Struck."

Claudine met his gaze with a bland smile. Earlier she'd told me she and her husband had been living amicably apart for the last ten years, in apartments a two-kilometer walk from each other and equidistant from their daughter's school. Before the girl was born, Claudine's romantic feelings for her husband had been strong, but soon after, they morphed into something fraternal, more affection than attraction, as if the child was, to both of them, the little sister that neither, being only children, had ever had. We're like siblings when we're together, she said. We play a lot, go on trips, amuse ourselves in many ways. And when I'm alone, yes, I go on dates, I have affairs. American men tended to bore her with their practicality, but she always held out hope that during a conference or a retreat such as this, she could meet someone who aroused her interest enough to have a bit of fun.

Giving up eating animals as a teenager, Bradley said, was the greatest act of change he'd ever committed, greater even than leaving the church. His parents had watched him bring foods into the house they had no idea existed: fermented legumes, sprouted grains, cultured nut milks. They would watch him prepare his own dinner as if he were a wizard stirring potions on the stove, and they'd wonder aloud how he summoned enough energy to make it through the day, how he ever felt properly full. Most people assume it's a moral compulsion that made me give up meat, but really I just wanted to differentiate myself. I ate dinner one night at a friend's house, his entire family was vegan, and just like that I was transformed. It wasn't even that I particularly liked what they were eating, it was that I saw for the first time, here's this alternative, interesting way to live—so why not? Some people—guys especially—need to mark their territory by planting a flag on a mountaintop, or stringing, whatever it was, seven thousand flags across Central Park, or peeing strategically on a tree. I've never been interested in that sort of thing. Some people need to go around making sure everybody knows they're vegan and how they came to be vegan and how everybody needs to be vegan, but for me it's always just been a personal decision. Like a trip to an interesting place, where I ended up staying because I got an enormous kick out of knowing it existed and that I'd discovered it. At first, the taste of plants nauseated me. I'd encountered them only in the presence of meat and cheese before—even a green salad in my parents' home had bits of bacon. All I could taste when I ate a spinach leaf was dirty water. I pictured myself drinking from a puddle, chewing on algae, my insides slimy. For about a week I sat around ill and nauseated, my digestive tract a complete mess. And then, practically overnight, my cravings reversed themselves: I spent the next twelve years feeling no desire for foods that used to be my staples.

He'd run marathons, he went on, and hiked the Appalachian Trail on a vegan diet. He drank his coffee black and found that butter was not indispensable in the making of cakes or cookies. At barbecues he'd bring his own animal-free burgers and sausages. He never saw it as his mission to convert anyone, but he'd persuaded, unintentionally, a dozen or so people to abandon their old ways of eating. Barbecues were where the persuasions happened. It would be hard, he acknowledged, to think of a more unsuitable place for a vegan than a Texas barbecue; there was more than one occasion where, had he not been a friend or family member of the host's, he would have been ejected from the property, but instead, people looked at him with pity and intrigue as he placed his offerings over the hot coals. Inevitably someone would ask for a bite, and as they chewed, their faces would light up with surprised approval. It was at one such barbecue where, although he'd brought his usual plant-based foods to grill, he became drawn, for the first time in over a decade, to the smell of steak. He remembered wondering if he was anemic, if his body was telling him he needed iron-rich blood. Or perhaps the craving was a spike of curiosity, the mirror image of what had inspired him to abandon meat and milk all those years prior. He helped himself to a T-bone. The guests stared in shock as he placed a forkful of flesh in his mouth. Some of them winced, as if they knew his body was not up to the task. It tasted strange, he remembered, as if one part of him remembered the taste exactly and another part had forgotten. That night he woke up breathless and sweating. He called for an ambulance, and by the time he got to the emergency room, he needed intravenous antihistamines. A tick bite he'd sustained months earlier was to blame, he learned later. The insect had circulated in his body a particle—of flesh, blood, or skin from a deer—priming his immune system to attack anything that resembled it. There was no cure, he was told. He had to be vegan for the rest of his life. Or basically vegan—no beef, no lamb, no pork, no venison, no dairy.

But that's easy for you, is it not? Claudine said. You've already developed the habit.

You just go back, Miguel added. Back to doing what you were doing.

Bradley looked at the ground. His jaw, scattered with the same wiry red hairs as his legs, clenched and released. There was no going back, he said. That piece of steak tasted of earth itself—as he'd chewed, he'd tasted the grass the animal consumed and the salts and minerals that constituted the grass, and he knew that he deserved to eat this flesh, was as a human being *made* to eat it, so it was terrible to learn right then that it would forever be denied to him, that he'd been deported, essentially, from the world of meat. He was living in exile.

Claudine and Miguel exchanged looks, and Bradley tapped his foot faster. He turned to me. Where did you say you live?

At the moment, I said, here.

But where's home for you?

My things are in storage for the summer. I have a place in Boston for August.

So you're moving to Boston.

No, I said, enjoying his confusion. I told him I'd been living there for almost a year. My things were just in storage for the summer.

Where were you before?

Pennsylvania.

That's where you grew up?

It's where I went to college.

But where did you *come* from?

From Boston. I took a bus to Portland.

I meant, where are you from? Originally. Where were you *born*?

I took pity and told him, and his face relaxed visibly. Never been there, he said and emptied his beer with a swallow. I've heard great things about it, though.

■

At dinner I sat across from Sheila, a writer who had spent ten years on her first book, a surrealistic novel, and was now working on her second, a memoir. Your life story will sell more easily than your fiction right now, her agent had said after the novel failed to land with a publisher; you're a Muslim living in post-9/11 America and that's the sort of story people are looking for these days—which only confirmed for her that Americans had no trouble embracing as reality all sorts of myths and fantasies while at the same time declaring their disdain for fiction. She wanted initially to resist her agent's advice but ended up giving in to this demand that the *I* in her writing refer indisputably to herself. At first the experience was degrading. She felt like the world's biggest liar, passing off memories as real events, and the world's biggest fool for assuming her personal life was of any interest to anyone. And then, when her agent sold the first chapter as a stand-alone piece to a magazine, she decided she must be the world's most successful con artist: she could write about factual things in spectacularly misleading ways and get people to drink it all up. Instead of luring them into a fictional dream, she ensnared them in a double fantasy: the story itself and then the illusion that it had happened. When the magazine piece was reprinted in an anthology, a publishing house offered a contract for her memoir without even waiting for the finished book. She used to be a slow writer, producing at most three paragraphs a week; these days, awareness of her newfound hypnotic powers brought surges of gleeful energy so strong she could type up to twenty pages in a single sitting. Thanks for sending me your novel chapter, she said now, in her perpetually tremulous voice. I printed it out and read it this morning. I enjoyed it, and didn't expect to, to be honest—the realist mode is usually not my thing—but your protagonist has been on my mind all day.

She helped herself to a piece of bread and passed me the basket. What had seemed extravagant to us on the first night—the three-course meal whose menu we were assured would never repeat during our stay, the double chandeliers suspended above the long wooden table and carved chairs, the cloth napkins, the antlered heads of moose surveying us from the walls—had already become routine. Sheila held the bread to her mouth with both hands, her thin arms bent like a praying mantis's. Streaks of silver ran through her hair, cut in long, straight bangs over her eyes, which were large and round, circled by thick smudges of kohl.

I recognized so much about your protagonist, she said: her Miss Goody Two-Shoes affect, always polite, always obliging, the way she addresses her elders with respect even when they're teasing and taunting and shaming her. That scene where she's ironing her uniform—yes, I remember doing the same, pressing those sleeve creases into blades, bleaching my socks, rubbing my shoes until that black fake leather gave off its own light, all to avoid incurring the wrath of my teachers, those nuns, oh how I recognized them, too. I still have this scar on my knuckle, see, from when Sister Elizabeth rapped me with a wooden ruler because of my handwriting. I must have been ten or eleven at the time. I remember her bearing down on me while I cowered in my chair and nursed my hand and prayed she wouldn't strike me again. And when I went home crying to my parents, they told me, the same way your protagonist's parents told her, that if I was punished in class, I must have done something to deserve it.

You went to a Catholic school? I asked.

She glared at me. Did you think we have only madrassas in Pakistan?

My impression, I said, was that her country's educational system had retained its British character to an even greater extent than had India's.

She laughed bitterly. Yes, either we're still British subjects or we're Islamists. As if the only language we understand is authoritarianism.

Her quavering voice had risen. I looked to see if others had noticed, but the rest of the table was paying rapt attention to Bradley's story of a writer whose latest work had suffered the indignity of being made not into a movie but a Broadway musical. The show's runaway success meant that the author's future projects, which would continue to be attempts at high literary form, would now be financed by a parody of his own work. There was no greater fall.

That cowering attitude of your protagonist, Sheila went on, I totally relate to it. That sense of being under siege. It's not just how I was as a child, but how I am as an adult, too, always trying to make myself invisible in the hopes that if I'm not noticed I'll be made to suffer less. Instead of fleeing a dangerous situation—or not getting into it in the first place—I sit there paralyzed, and let the blows rain down on me as if I deserve them. I read an article the other day about airplane evacuation drills. Apparently there are always a few people who remain in their seats, curled in fetal position with their seat belts buckled. A misplaced evolutionary impulse to play dead, useless when the situation demands rapid retreat. Your protagonist is that way, too.

I didn't see my protagonist as cowering at all, I replied. She was simply a quiet sort of kid.

No, it's more than that, Sheila said. That section when an adult tells her she's a good-for-nothing—instead of standing up for herself and saying, or at least thinking, No, I'm not, she retreats. I felt I understood her deeply in that moment, which is the only moment in the chapter when the focus is on her.

Our soup bowls were cleared away and replaced with plates of grilled fish. Sheila ate distractedly, her gaze fixed on a point somewhere to the side of her food. For the ten years she'd spent writing her novel, she said, she'd kept herself afloat by cobbling together various gigs: adjunct teaching, freelance editing, secretarial work. Her younger siblings, one a lawyer, the other an economist, had made their family proud; when her parents telephoned, it was always to express concern, to remind her, with their anxious questions, that she was a failure. The novel was meant to be her ticket out of all that. Rejection had brought on desperation, and in that state, she'd applied to all manner of entry-level positions with the word "writer" in them. Finance writer, science writer, blog writer: she marveled at these opportunities she'd never known existed, and had she been aware, she would have marched past them—I'm a *real* writer, I have no use for gigs like this—never thinking that one day she'd find herself knocking at those same doors, only to find them shutting in her face and opening for candidates in their twenties, aspiring poets and novelists with a spring in their step, who had the foresight to secure proper salaries and health insurance. She'd holed up with her novel for so long she was practically feral.

Are you giving me advice? I asked.

She spat into her napkin before pushing her plate away. Me of all people give advice. I'm more a walking cautionary tale of what not to do. She picked up her half-eaten slice of bread from where it lay on the tablecloth and resumed nibbling. In that state of desperation, she said—not for money so much as to prove she wasn't a failure—she unwittingly signed up for a job she wasn't suited to, and though she now acknowledged the experience had shaken something loose in her, some obstruction she'd never recognized, which kept her those ten years from writing directly about her life, she was still aghast at herself for not turning and fleeing at the first signs of danger. She'd known within minutes of meeting the man who'd become her boss, a consultant to various organizations, that there was something off about him, an air of annoyed discomfort, as if he was determined to ignore the malfunctioning organ that was pumping him full of venom. On the occasions he made eye contact with her or smiled, it was obvious that these gestures were the product of laborious train-ing, the way a person with no musical talent can produce, after years of practice, a tune that's technically correct though devoid of any feel-ing or spontaneity. He must have decided at a young age, because he had no friends in school and was constantly embarrassing himself at social occasions, to conquer his problem of relating to people—and then made a career of the conquest. Every day, Sheila watched how multiple times and for hundreds of dollars an hour he doled out to clients the sort of advice he had trouble following himself: how to gain people's trust, how to listen to and persuade and manage one's colleagues. He sat, walked, and spoke like a robot. She never saw him without his headset on and flashing. He could talk with one client while typing an email to another. I have to keep growing the com-pany, he told her. Your job is to create the impression that I'm more available to clients than I really am.

Sheila dropped her head into her hands. Her body was shaking, from sobs, I assumed, but when she straightened up, her face was dry and there was a new light in her enormous eyes. What sort of idiot, she said shrilly, what sort of imbecile says yes to a job like that? With a guy who's clearly beyond help? He needed a punching bag, not an assistant, someone he could treat in all the ways he'd trained himself not to treat his clients. I'd ask him a question, and he'd tell me I was stupid; I'd spend hours writing a report, and all he'd notice was the inconsequent detail I got wrong. In his emails to me, the most violent emails I've ever received, he'd sign off "Warmly," a word that now gives me the heebie-jeebies every time I hear it. I never worked up the courage to defend myself; I just let him flog me. Be bold, I want to tell your protagonist. People who make you feel small are people you should avoid.

Dessert was being handed around. Sheila abandoned her crust of bread and added several spoons of sugar to her coffee. I couldn't help thinking, she said, that a rupture between your protagonist and her family is inevitable, if she's to see them for who they are. There's a palpable distance between her and the reader, which mirrors, I think, the distance she feels from the people around her. I found myself thinking, Either some external event is going to shake this girl out of her shyness and force her to act, or the resentment she just has to be bottling up, toward her mother, her family, at this whole Bangalore society she's trapped in, will erupt.

My goal, I said, was to have her be an observer, a Nick Carraway sort, present but always peripheral.

I don't see her as peripheral at all, Sheila said. She's our conduit to the world of the book, which is exclusively *her* world and therefore an extension of herself.

I wanted to say that by peripheral I meant she wasn't directly involved in the main events, but I suspected whatever I said would only prolong our argument and add to the damage that these observations of my protagonist had already caused to my confidence in the novel, so I said nothing.

Sheila and I ate our slices of pie without speaking, exchanging wary looks across the table. How has your experience been here? she asked at last. She personally found retreats like these frustrating. She set impossible goals, and then writer's block would set in by the second or third day. It hadn't this time, though. Not yet at least. After the consultant fired her, she realized the only thing she was fit for was to go back to her cave and write. She put down her coffee and flailed her skinny arms like a Bollywood heroine about to faint. Something needed to strike me, you see, something out of the blue. The way a nuclear bomb blows atoms apart and lets loose their energy.

CHAPTER SEVENTEEN

On the Concord Trailways bus, the woman in the seat beside me tapped her knuckle to the window. Spectacular slowdown this, she said. Like a border crossing in wartime. We could be hours away, days for all we know, and it's anyone's guess what state the world will be in by the time we arrive.

Moments later, the driver's voice addressed us from the speakers. An overturned oil tanker was to blame for the backup, he said cheerily, and the rain wasn't helping. The goal was still to get us all to Boston safely and as speedily as possible.

My neighbor asked if I had a phone charger she could borrow—her own, which she'd purchased in this country specifically for traveling, refused to fit in the outlet beside us. With her long face and somber clothes, she seemed British in a classic sort of way: an English governess out of a Brontë novel. Her quick smile showed broad, straight teeth, and I was reminded of my mother's unfailing remark whenever footage of the British royals appeared on television, that the English looked exactly like the horses they were so obsessed with. My neighbor plugged my charger into the outlet and examined the connector. Oh dear, she said, I don't believe this will fit my phone. She unplugged the cord, wrapped it briskly and neatly, and returned it to me. I'm sorry, dear, would you mind if I borrowed your phone for a moment? Just one quick call? Thank you so much. She tapped haltingly at the keypad. It's been a while since I used this model—is this the call button here, this green one?

I pressed it for her, and as she reclined with my device to her ear and her head turned discreetly away from me, I looked past her to the rain lashing the pane of glass, the droplets darting over the surface in the wind. If I craned my neck, I could see the cars below, all at a standstill, and a broad river of traffic meandering into the distance. We were stopped in the middle of alternating meadow and woods, various shades of green obscured by mist, and I wondered whether my neighbor, if she was indeed from England, felt at home in this dreary landscape, which I imagined bore some resemblance to the Yorkshire moors. I sat back and went through my travel documents. The school's lawyer had provided a list, and I checked my papers against it for the fifth or sixth time that day. The mood in the bus was turning restless. This does not look good, a man's voice said from the row behind. This does not look good at all, it's a freakin' parking lot. I reminded myself there was still plenty of time: my flight was more than four hours off, and we'd already crossed the border into Massachusetts.

The Englishwoman returned the phone and thanked me. She'd left a voicemail, she said, for friends who were planning to drive to the airport to meet her, telling them not to come—there'd be no time for the drink they'd planned.

Where was she flying to? I asked.

England, she said. She'd been to Maine to see her son and daughter-in-law, who'd just had a baby. And you? she asked, twisting sideways to face me more comfortably. Are you traveling beyond Boston?

India, I said. Via England.

Ah, she said, my birthplace.

Where in England were you born?

Not England, she said. India. Tamil Nadu. I lived in Chennai—it was Madras back then of course—until I was seventeen. She settled her hands, which were long and elegant, in her lap—less a Jane Eyre or Agnes Grey, now that I knew she was from, in a sense, India, than a stately Mrs. Moore riding a tonga to the Marabar Caves.

Had she visited India since? I asked.

Oh yes, many times. And my parents just moved back there, not to Madras—the heat would be too much for them now, they're in their eighties—but Bangalore.

That's such a coincidence. Madras was my birthplace, too, and Bangalore my hometown.

Ah, she said again. You'll know it much better than I do, then. My recent trips have been mostly to Delhi, to these conferences where my organization is forever wanting me to present. The last time I was in Bangalore, I must have been about eleven years old. 1950, I'd say. I remember we took the train from Madras. I have so many memories of traveling across India by coach. For a time I thought it was one of the few good things we left India with, the railways.

On that Bangalore trip, she continued, her mother had wanted to find the grave of a great-uncle of hers, one of the first British officials to come to that city. He'd died from cholera. They arrived at a sprawling cemetery and spent hours searching for her great-great-uncle's headstone. She had this distinct memory, because of what happened next, of stamping her foot and crying to her father that she was tired and wanted to go home, and him saying to her, Just a little longer, Jenny, be patient now. They turned a corner and found themselves face to face with a cobra. A black, coiled thing, she said, hood flared, tongue flicking in and out—it was probably no higher than my knee, but when I picture it, it's as tall as I am, looking me straight in the eye, in the midst of headstones—graves of my countrymen, hundreds of them, maybe thousands, who'd sailed there as part of the vast, terrible project of empire. I didn't fully understand it at the time, but I felt a deep stirring, as if mixed in with my fear of that snake was a fear of something much larger, this awful enterprise I was implicated in and would be made to pay for in due course.

Her childhood in India, up to that moment, had been nothing short of idyllic. Her parents, both trained in theater, ran an arts program in the backyard of their bungalow, under a tree, Santiniketan style. They'd come to India six months after Independence, by which time there were few British people left in Madras, a fact that suited her mother and father very well. They wanted nothing more than to live among the locals, show them, as she remembered her father saying once, that we, meaning the British, don't bite—or no longer bite. He was of the generation who believed that India was still part of Britain, a poor relation of sorts, who'd moved out of the family home but with whom decency required connections be maintained. We've come a long way together, he liked to say, as if colonization had been any sort of equal partnership. Growing up, she'd found it easy to assume—or pretend—she was an Indian girl. All her companions were Indian—in fact, the man who'd planned to meet her for tea at Logan was one of those childhood friends, now a pharmaceutical engineer settled in Waltham. Every two or three years, when her parents had taken her to England, her relatives were horrified by her freckles and tanned skin and what they considered "coolie" ways: eating with her fingers, running around barefoot. Cold, stern, and boring her mother country was, in contrast to hot, fun, sweaty India. The bungalow was a short distance from the ocean, and every evening she and her brother would run to the beach to watch the fishing boats come in. She remembered the sands as quite clean, the water always warm, and the smells of fish mixing with fresh flowers and boiled groundnuts from the open-air market. The area had since grown crowded and filthy, she'd heard, which was one reason she'd avoided traveling south on her recent trips to the country. She would always feel—that part of her still a child—that the white-sand beach, the bungalow with its backyard shaded by lime trees, that tiny piece of Madras, was indisputably hers, that it belonged to her and she to it. Good lord, she said, tapping the window. Here's something I never thought I'd see in this part of the world.

I leaned toward the glass. Traffic was still unmoving, the rain had lightened to a drizzle, and people were strolling along the side of the interstate as if it were a walking path through the mist. A woman leaned against the open door of her car, eating out of a Tupperware box while a group of teenagers sat nearby on a guardrail and posed for photographs.

I wish I had my camera, Jenny said. It's as if any moment we might see hawkers selling samosas and kulfi and chai. Or lychees, like they do in Thailand. But what I do see, oh dear, is a woman relieving herself behind those trees. She probably thinks she's hidden from view, poor thing.

Her mention of her parents' arts program, I said, reminded me of a theater production I'd joined in on as a high schooler: *Romeo and Juliet*, performed with Indian costumes, music, and dance sequences. I'd had a minor nonspeaking role, nothing more, but the whole experience had made me feel part of something large and good at a time when I was spending most of my after-school hours alone, studying for exams.

Ah, yes, theater is life and life theater, is it not? She resettled herself and crossed her knees, which were clad in dark leggings that shone like silk. She smiled, the wrinkles around her eyes and mouth full of humor and kindness. I'd like to think my parents did a measure of good with their little program. Certainly the children and families were very grateful, and I just remember the bungalow being such a lively place, with costumes and papier-mâché props everywhere and kids singing in chorus or reciting their lines.

How long had her parents kept the program going? I asked.

Seventeen years, she said. They'd have kept it active for the rest of their lives if they'd had a choice.

I waited for her to elaborate, but she seemed preoccupied by a thought. Her wide brow was furrowed as she traced the hem of her skirt. We were lurching forward, the mass of vehicles finally on the move. I opened my folder and perused my papers again. By the time I looked up, the halting motions of the bus had given way to something steadier. When I sensed we were turning I craned my neck, but all that was visible past the orange cones and a man in a fluorescent vest directing us off the highway was a wall of fire engines and police cars, lights blazing through the wetness, hiding from view whatever mishap had caused the delay.

Seems like we're on our way now, my neighbor said. She sounded cheerful again, no longer preoccupied, and was sitting erect, her hands clasped around one knee. I wonder if we're on the same flight before you go on to Bangalore? And perhaps if you give me your email address, I can introduce you to my parents? They'd love to have you over for tea. They're still a bit lonely, I think—it's not easy for them to adjust to being back in India, and I won't have time to visit until Christmas at the earliest. Here. She delved in her handbag, which had, like her clothes, a sophisticated, austere look, and pulled out a large sealed envelope. These are some photographs of the baby. I was going to put them in the post, but I've a feeling they're far more likely to reach their destination safe and sound if you take them. There's my parents' Bangalore address, as you'll see. I cannot tell you how delighted they'll be if you show up at their door with pictures of their great-grandson and say you and I met on a bus—they'll take you in as family. Will you, please? And let me give you my card.

I accepted both. Emergency aid, she said, in response to my reading aloud the name of her organization, whose logo sat alongside the laureled polar grid of the United Nations. Disaster zones, war zones, that's where we go, places where the absolute basics are needed: water, blankets, medicines. Much simpler than what my parents set out to do. They—we, I should say, for my brother and I were as devoted to the theater program as they were—we all had such a sense of purpose, it was impossible for us to imagine such a thing wouldn't be appreciated by everyone else. And then the moment came, as it does in everyone's life, I suppose, when you realize that the little stage, and the events upon it that you consider your life, is but a play within a much larger play. A former student of her parents, a Tamilian boy they considered so prodigiously talented that they wrote to a friend of theirs at Cambridge recommending he be admitted as a student of English, returned—years later—with his degree and a new, angry light in his eyes. Her parents were expecting stories of what a wonderful, inspiring time he'd had in England, but instead he pushed aside the cake her mother had baked to celebrate the occasion of his return and embarked on a diatribe that in the decades since had played over and over in Jenny's head. She could still see his face, the hollows of his cheeks illuminated by candlelight—the electricity must have been out. He had a gravelly, resonant voice, the sort that fills a room and makes the hair stand on the back of your neck. I can feel no gratitude toward you, he told my parents, because you—you British—continue to destroy me. You don't know how to stop. Existence as you know it is based upon my annihilation, the destruction of my history, my lands, my language. You come to this ground as if you are welcome, you make brown children recite the words of dead white men, which we readily do because we think—have been made to think—it will bestow on us some measure of the superiority that you so graciously represent. The damage goes far beyond your killings and looting; you've twisted my mind so that when I look in the mirror I see a subhuman creature, dark, small, subservient. It doesn't matter how much I remind myself of my country's glories—that the lands whose borders you drew without regard to the interests of the people who inhabit them, those lands that are now called India, were once the wealthiest and most prosperous in the world—or how the knowledge enshrined in the Vedas predates so many of your Western discoveries, that your Greek mythologies have not a shred of the complexity and sophistication of my Indian epics—that we are now a free country, free to chart our own destiny. None of it matters; I will continue to be chained like a dog, heaving against my restraints, snapping at a piece of meat just beyond my reach, chafing my neck, choking myself in the process. I'll go on straining to imitate you, to speak your language, to adapt your ways as mine, and thereby remain imprisoned. The following night, Jenny said, a mob descended—it was during a production of *The Importance of Being Earnest*—and burned down the house. Nobody was hurt, fortunately, and it was never determined who exactly was responsible, but that was the end of our stay in Madras.

The bus had picked up speed, and our driver announced we'd reach Logan in ten minutes.

Are you sure, my neighbor asked, that it won't be too much trouble for you to meet my parents? They'd love it—they'd warm to you immediately. It's been more than thirty years since Madras, since we all left, and though they were eager to return to India, I can imagine they're also a little wary. It would do them good to meet someone like you, a kind stranger whose path crossed with mine, but I don't want to inconvenience you if you're busy.

I said it would be no trouble at all, that I'd be glad to deliver the photographs and spend some time with her parents. I considered them brave to return in their old age to India, and I hoped that they could look forward to a relatively peaceful time.

The bus pulled to the curb outside our terminal, and as we disembarked into the cold, wet wind, I hugged my folder, with its important papers, to my chest. Inside the revolving door, as my neighbor and I entered the same line for check-in, I asked if she considered England her home.

No, she said. It's the mother country, but not home really.

Where was home then?

Nowhere, I suppose. More and more these days I have the sense of belonging nowhere, that all I do is move among places and times. I board a flight in Boston and close my eyes, and when I open them, I'm in London or Port-au-Prince or Addis Ababa. Or I'm a child again, in Madras. I must be a tortoise. Home is my life, everything that I've seen and been, and it just comes along with me. Do you know what I mean?

I think so, I said before we were called to separate counters.

Where are you going today? the airline representative asked me.

I handed over my passport and watched her eyelashes, shined with mascara, rise and fall as she compared my face to my photograph. Your ticket says you're going to London, she said.

I'm not going to London. I'm going to Bangalore.

You're routed through London.

Through Heathrow, I said. I'm not spending any time in London.

To enter London, you'll need a visa for the UK. Do you have one?

I won't be entering London. I'll just be in the airport.

You'll need a transit visa to go through London.

I pushed my sheaf of documents toward her. I'm in OPT status. I have an appointment in India to get a new American visa. But it shouldn't matter—I'm an Indian citizen traveling on an Indian passport.

She thumbed through my papers and shook her head. I'm afraid I can't let you through. For someone in your circumstances, since you hold a passport from one of these countries—she brandished a printed list—the new regulations require a transit visa. For the UK, France, Germany, I believe all of Europe at this point.

I collected my documents with clammy hands. Through the ringing in my ears, I heard the woman say that unfortunately, since I didn't have travel insurance, my ticket would not be refunded. I stepped away, fumbled for my cell phone, and called the number listed for the school's lawyer. A man's voice said hello, and I tried to explain what had just happened.

Well, he said and cleared his throat, from what I'm seeing in your file, your OPT status has expired.

But I had the document certifying it had been extended, I said.

He wasn't the one assigned to my case, he said, but from the notes he was looking at, I had already overstayed my visa.

I repeated that my paperwork was in order and that no one had told me I'd need special permission to fly through Europe.

Overstaying your visa constitutes unlawful presence.

I scanned the vast terminal like a fugitive. My legs felt unsteady, my mouth dry as I found a seat and dialed another number, this time with the calling card I hadn't taken out of my wallet in weeks. My mother picked up on the third ring. What happened? she demanded in Tamil. Why are you telephoning?

I'd run into some problems at the airport, I said. I'd need to buy another ticket, through Dubai or some other non-European city, and I didn't have the money.

How can they make you buy another ticket? she wanted to know. How can they not let you board the plane? In the background I heard a dog barking and the musical horn of a lorry. Everybody's still sleeping, my mother said. I'll call the travel agent later.

Ma, I don't have a place to spend the night. My voice was suddenly hoarse. I'm trying to come back. Please can you help me get home?

Acknowledgments

My OPT sponsor, for everything they taught me.

Early readers, who encouraged me to keep going: Awa Diop, Sara Freeman, Soo Yeon Hong, Shilpi Suneja. Late readers, who caught my blind spots: Viplav Saini, Lisa Harries Schumann, Sujata Shekar.

Sarah Burnes, my trusted agent. Yuka Igarashi, my wise and generous editor. The talented staff at Graywolf Press for treating my work with such care and respect.

The podcast *Scene on Radio*, whose episode on Bhagat Singh Thind inspired the opening from which this novel unspooled.

And my love, Bill Pierce, who listened to each chapter, and read, and listened.

SHUBHA SUNDER is the author of *Boomtown Girl*, a story collection set in her hometown of Bangalore, India, that won the 2021 St. Lawrence Book Award. She lives in Boston, Massachusetts, with her family.

Graywolf Press publishes risk-taking, visionary writers who transform culture through literature. As a nonprofit organization, Graywolf relies on the generous support of its donors to bring books like this one into the world.

This publication is made possible, in part, by the voters of Minnesota through a Minnesota State Arts Board Operating Support grant, thanks to a legislative appropriation from the arts and cultural heritage fund. Significant support has also been provided by other generous contributions from foundations, corporations, and individuals. To these supporters we offer our heartfelt thanks.

To learn more about Graywolf's books and authors or make a tax-deductible donation, please visit www.graywolfpress.org.

The text of *Optional Practical Training* is set in Adobe Jenson Pro.
Book design by Rachel Holscher.
Composition by Bookmobile Design & Digital
Publisher Services, Minneapolis, Minnesota.
Manufactured by Friesens on acid-free,
100 percent postconsumer wastepaper.